Flint and Steele Mysteries

The Mattress Affair

Cheryl Landmark

For your enjoyment!
Cheryl Landmark

DEDICATION

To all my sweet, loyal, and loving fur children, past and present, who are all as intelligent and clever as Flint

Baron, Destiny, Misty, Faye and Kitty

ACKNOWLEDGMENTS

A big thank you to Stacey Coverstone, my wonderful editor who worked diligently with me to ensure this book is the best it can be.

Prologue

My name is Flint, a.k.a. The Nose. And I'm a detective; a pretty doggone good detective, too, if I do say so myself. And I *can* say so because I really am a dog—a four-year-old black Labrador retriever, to be exact. My partner is a very nice human named Meredith Steele. Yeah, you guessed it. Our detective agency is called Flint and Steele. Pretty clever, wouldn't you say? Meredith couldn't resist giving me my unusual name when I came to her as a chubby eight-week-old pup. She thought it was catchy and made us a great sounding team, and she was right.

We live in a picturesque little place called Gros Cap, just west of the city of Sault Ste. Marie in Northern Ontario, which is in Canada. Our quaint log bungalow is built at the end of a long narrow gravel road on the shore

1

of the St. Mary's River where it empties out into Whitefish Bay and Lake Superior. When some of those howling Northern Ontario winter blizzards sweep across the lake into the bay, there are times when it can seem like we're stuck in the middle of the Arctic tundra. But we don't really mind. Meredith just stokes up the airtight woodstove until it's crackling with cheery flames and we watch in cozy, warm comfort from the living room windows as the snowstorms block out the sight of the shipping channel and Little Dog Island.

Our nearest neighbor, whose house is also on the same road as ours but out of sight, is a feisty old lady named Abigail Tunner, who claims she's sixty years old, but I'm pretty sure she's closer to seventy-five. Even so, she's a tough old bird, that Abigail, and still pretty spry for her age. Cuts her own firewood, does all the maintenance work around her house and yard, plants a vegetable garden every spring and makes her own preserves, jams and jellies.

Abigail claims to be descended from the Ojibwa natives who used to live around this area back in the early 1800s, and I believe her. She certainly seems to have an affinity for nature and the land that the First Nations people have always had. As for her assertion that she can sometimes talk with the spirits of the land and the water, I'm not too sure about that, although it wouldn't surprise me in the least.

Her granddaddy, Albert Tunner, built the log house in Gros Cap nearly eighty years ago. It started out originally as a simple one-room cabin, but over the years, it grew into a sturdy, two-story house with plenty of rustic charm and character. Abigail's parents used it as a summer cottage, preferring to live the rest of the year in the city of Sault Ste. Marie instead of out in the wilderness. But when Abigail inherited the place thirty years ago, she moved out to Gros Cap permanently. She never married—Meredith says she's just too stubborn and ornery for any man to put up with for long—and has always lived alone in the big log house. I remember Abigail once saying she would sooner talk to the trees, the rocks and the wolves than some of the people she encounters. As for me, I like humans most of the time and Meredith all of the time, but I think I can understand Abigail's feelings toward some of the, shall we say, less *desirable* examples of humankind.

Despite Abigail's apparent aversion to the company of others, for some reason she's decided that Meredith and I don't fall into that category and honors us with a visit every now and then or an invitation to her house. Occasionally, she'll even give us some of her freshly baked bread or homemade blueberry jam. But of course, she never admits these are social visits. That would ruin her image as the resident cantankerous hermit of Gros Cap.

Meredith seems to like the old lady and takes little offense at her diatribes. My human is pretty perceptive and I think she, like me, can see right through Abigail's testy attitude. Whenever she thinks Meredith isn't looking, the old lady scratches my ears and slips me tasty bits of dried beef jerky she makes herself. Now that, to me, is proof-positive there lurks a nice human being under that crusty exterior!

The bungalow my partner and I live in is a bit smaller than Abigail's house, but no less charming and rustic. The floor in the living room is oak hardwood with a couple of nice leaf-motif area rugs scattered here and there. My favorite one lies right in front of the woodstove where I can stretch out for a pleasant nap on cold winter evenings or on the long, lazy dog days of summer. The house faces the bay and huge windows afford magnificent views of it. Meredith has thoughtfully provided me with a comfortable chair right in front of one of them, so I can keep a lookout for squirrels and bunny rabbits in the yard. The kitchen is small but cozy and boasts lovely pine cupboards and counters and cheery yellow curtains at the windows.

Okay, enough background information. You're probably asking yourself why a dog calls himself a detective. Well, ever since last summer, I've discovered that I have a natural aptitude for the job, as well as a keen interest in solving mysteries.

You see, what happened last August was that three-year old Kylie Morrison went missing. She just disappeared from the yard when her mother went into the house to get some lemonade. Greg and Judy Morrison live a couple of houses down the shoreline from where Meredith and I do. A frantic search for the child ensued, with several neighbors joining in. Yours truly was among the search party, and as you can probably guess, I found Kylie about two hours after the search began. She had wandered off chasing colorful butterflies and had somehow ended up inside a ravine with numerous deadfalls and tangled brush blocking it. My sensitive hearing picked up her frightened whimpers from the bottom of the ravine and I slipped down the bank where I found her standing by a fallen log, tears streaming down her dirt-streaked face. At first, my sudden appearance frightened her, but when she realized I was a dog and not some wild animal about to attack her, a smile struggled through the tears and her eyes lit up.

"Doggie!" she cried, running over to hug my neck tightly.

She appeared to be uninjured but thoroughly frightened, and I was able to bring her up and out of the ravine with her clinging tightly to my collar.

I was hailed a hero and given ear scratches and pats on the head by the grateful parents and relieved searchers. That evening, back at our house, Meredith rewarded me with extra treats and hugs and told me how proud she was of me. To be honest, I didn't really consider myself a hero, just a dog doing his natural duty of protecting and rescuing helpless little children. But I have to say, the experience did give me a thrill of satisfaction and a sense of accomplishment.

After that incident came the one with Joe and Linda Ford, the electrician and his wife who live at the beginning of our gravel road just off Second Line West. One afternoon, their shed was broken into and a number of items stolen, including an MP3 player that Joe had left on his workbench.

That evening, while I was over at their place paying a visit to their Jack Russell terrier, Geordie, my sensitive nose picked up two unfamiliar scents around the shed. I tried to enlist Geordie's help in finding out where the trail led, but the silly young pup was more interested in chasing chipmunks. Leaving him to his panting pursuits, I followed the scents to a neighboring cottage on the next road over from us, which had recently been purchased by a couple with two teenaged sons. Lo and behold, I discovered the stolen loot hidden under the back deck.

Crawling into the dark space, I retrieved the MP3 player and carried it in my mouth to the Ford's house. Joe opened the patio door in response to my urgent scratching, saw the MP3 player, and immediately recognized it as his stolen one because it had a piece of black electrical tape covering a small crack on the back of it. When I made it obvious that I wanted him to follow me, he did and I led him to the rest of the stolen goodies.

Faced with the incontrovertible evidence, the two young boys confessed, and I was rewarded for my deductive work with a nice juicy steak from the grateful Fords. The only downside was that I had to share the steak with Geordie, even though the little mutt didn't help solve the case. But since he's my best buddy, I didn't mind sharing too much.

Next came the case of the missing hunter up on Marshall Drive...but I think you get my drift.

The neighbors began to laughingly refer to me as Detective Flint, or The Nose, and that gave me the idea of putting my canine gifts of excellent smell and hearing to good use. Thus, I decided to open up the detective agency of Flint and Steele, although I'm not sure Meredith realizes I've recruited her as my partner in the enterprise. I haven't offered Geordie a partnership in my investigative firm though, despite my friendship with him. I don't think he has it in him to be a good detective—the scamp's just a little too immature and scatterbrained—and besides, the name *Flint and Steele and Geordie* just doesn't have quite the right ring to it.

Anyway, since I've captured your attention, I'd like to tell you about a case involving our elderly neighbor Abigail. This mystery requiring my sleuthing skills turned out to be the deadliest one so far in the case files of the Flint and Steele agency.

Chapter 1

He's coming, blast him!"

Meredith gasped and nearly dropped the box of groceries she was carrying as the disembodied voice bellowed out from the dim shadows of the roofed porch. Following closely on her heels up the steps, I let out a startled yelp at the sudden loud words.

Meredith peered into the gloom. "Abby?"

"Well, it sure ain't Mother Teresa, girlie! Who else do you think would be sitting on my porch?"

Meredith blew out her breath in an exasperated sigh. "Good lord, Abigail, you nearly gave me a heart attack. What the heck are you doing skulking in the shadows?"

The old lady snorted and I could dimly make out her hunched figure sitting in the wooden rocking chair in the far corner of the porch. "I'm not skulking," she said, huffily. "I'm sitting on my own porch minding my own business, where I have every right to be."

Meredith sighed and set the box of groceries on a small rickety table beside the screen door. "Okay, okay, never mind. What did you mean by he's coming? Who's coming?"

Abigail stood up abruptly, sending the old rocking chair into violent, creaking motion. "Caleb, blast him, that good-for-nothing boy and his shrill harpy of a wife! I told him I didn't want him here, but would he listen to me? No, of course not, he's as pig-headed and dense as his father."

Meredith looked mystified as Abigail paced furiously back and forth along the porch. I had to back hastily out of the way to avoid having my front paws trod on.

"Who's Caleb?"

The old lady threw her a glance but never slowed her angry pacing. "My useless nephew, that's who. He called me this afternoon. He and his wife Rowena want to come up here and spend a week with me. Can you believe that? A whole week!" Her hazel eyes snapped. "They're city folk from Toronto. Why in blazes do they want to come up here to the bush and spend a week with a crazy old lady?"

"You're not crazy, just eccentric," Meredith said. Her green eyes shone with curiosity. "You've never mentioned a nephew before. I didn't even know you had brothers or sisters."

"Well, it's not something I go around bragging about," Abigail grumbled. "Caleb is my brother Ronald's son. Ronald and his wife Minnie live in Mississauga, which, as far as I'm concerned, is still not far enough away from me."

At Meredith's raised eyebrow, the old lady snorted with disdain. "Ronald and I never got along very well when we were growing up. I always thought he was a sissy, a real momma's boy. I could make him cry just by showing him a worm." Her wrinkled face twisted with glee. "I remember the time I shoved a frog down the back of his shirt in front of Ginny Smithers. You should have heard the girlie squeals that came out of that boy as he jumped around trying to get that frog out! He never forgave me for that."

Meredith tried to look stern but couldn't quite hide the amused twitch of her lips. "Now, Abigail Tunner, that was cruel. Poor Ronald."

Abigail grinned unrepentantly. "It served him right for being such a baby. Anyway, things haven't changed much over the years. I still think Ronald's a wimp and he still thinks I'm a big bully, as well as crazy for living up here in the bush. He even called me a nutty old hermit once. Well, in my opinion, he's even crazier to live in all that concrete and traffic and smog. We don't stay in touch much, maybe a phone call every now and then. Since our parents died, he and Minnie haven't been up to visit, and that suits me just fine."

"And Caleb? Do you have much contact with him?"

"Hah! Are you kidding? That boy is as bad as his father, wimpy and useless. He's thirty-eight years old and still can't keep a job for more than a year or two. And that wife of his rules the roost, no doubt about that. She's one of those uppity women who think they're so much better than everyone else and entitled to have everything handed to them on a silver platter. I can't stand the woman and I only met her once."

"Oh, well, then, that's plenty of time to form an accurate impression," Meredith said, dryly.

Abigail glowered at her. "I know what my eyes and ears and gut instincts tell me, girlie. That woman is no good and Caleb should realize that, but then I didn't really expect any offspring of Ronald's to have much in the way of the brain department." She pointed at me. "Flint there has more intelligence than the two of them put together."

I perked up my ears, pleased by the compliment, especially coming from an old woman who handed out compliments as readily as she would money to complete strangers on the street.

Abigail resumed her furious pacing. "Why in the devil's name do those two want to come here now, when they know I can't stand people, especially people who are unfortunately related to me."

"Maybe Caleb just wants to get to know you better," Meredith said, helpfully. "You know, mend the rift before it's too late."

Abigail sent her a disgusted look. "Hah! I'll believe that when I see pigs fly." Her expression turned sly. "Anyway, if you think I'm just being a foolish old woman who doesn't know what she's talking about, you can find out for yourself just what kind of people they are."

Meredith suddenly looked wary. "What do you mean?"

"They should get here around suppertime tomorrow, which is *another* thing that has me ticked off! They didn't even have the decency to give me proper notice that they were going to barge in on me."

"They probably didn't want to give you time to run away," Meredith said.

Abigail grunted sourly and then gave her a crafty glance. "Anyway, I want you to be here when they arrive and stay for supper with us."

"Now, Abby, I don't know if that's such a good idea. I'm sure they'd rather not have a complete stranger intruding on their first day here..."

"You're coming and that's it. No argument," the old lady said. "I don't intend to put up with those two by myself. I need moral support and, unfortunately, girlie, you're the person who's going to give it to me whether you want to or not. And bring Flint along, too. Maybe he can bite them if they get too obnoxious."

She cackled and picked up the box of groceries, disappearing into the house with it as the screen door banged loudly behind her. Meredith and I stared after her with identical flabbergasted expressions.

After a moment, my human sighed and crouched down to scratch behind my ears. "Well, Flint, old fellow, this should prove to be a very interesting visit."

I silently agreed.

Despite my conviction that Abigail often exaggerated her grouchy old woman act just to provoke reactions from other people and not really because she despised humankind, I had the distinct impression that she really didn't like her own family. If Caleb Tunner and his wife, Rowena, lasted even one day with the old lady, I would have been greatly surprised. And because I felt sorry for their upcoming ordeal, I vowed not to bite them, not even to please Abigail, the giver of secret treats.

Chapter 2

The next evening, Meredith and I headed toward Abigail's house along the narrow, pine needle-strewn path that ran between our two properties near the shoreline. My human partner appeared to be somewhat nervous at the upcoming meeting with Abigail's relatives. I could tell by the way she babbled on and on as she dragged her feet reluctantly along the sun-dappled path and stopped frequently to stare blindly out over the bay shimmering through the trees.

"They're probably not as bad as she says they are. You know how she is. Even if the poor man wore a halo, she would say it wasn't polished brightly enough or it was sitting crooked! Her brother Ronald is right--she *is* a big bully sometimes. Look how she browbeat *us* into coming tonight! But even so, I don't believe she's really malicious or cruel. I think she just gets a kick out of her reputation as the 'crazy old lady of Gros Cap'. Anyway, I just hope she doesn't harass the poor man and his wife too much. I don't relish the thought of having to be peacemaker between them, or having to mop up any blood if it comes to fisticuffs."

Meredith's nervous tirade finally trailed off like a tape recorder reaching the end of its tape, and she sighed, running her fingers through her short-cropped chestnut hair. "Flint, how do we get ourselves into these things?"

I looked up into her anxious face and whined softly, letting her know I sympathized with her feelings. With Abigail's penchant for tyranny, it was likely to be a very uncomfortable evening.

When we arrived at Abigail's log house at six o'clock, it appeared that Caleb and his wife had not yet arrived. Loud thumping sounds came from behind the house, and, curious, Meredith and I followed them to find the old lady chopping firewood with a grim-faced vengeance. She wore her usual attire of a man's plaid shirt tucked into faded blue jeans and a red handkerchief tied around her short curly gray hair.

Even though I was pretty sure she knew we were standing there, she steadfastly refused to acknowledge us and just kept right on chopping firewood like she was lopping off the heads of demonical beasts. Or perhaps, unwelcome nephews and their wives.

Meredith put her hands on her hips. "Abigail Tunner, what in heaven's name are you doing?"

The axe rose and fell with a vicious swoop that sent the two halves of a log flying halfway across the yard.

Abigail grunted. "Are you blind, girlie? Can't you see I'm knitting a sweater? What in blazes does it look like I'm doing?"

Meredith's pretty face assumed a patient expression. "Why are you chopping firewood in the middle of July when your nephew is due to arrive any minute?"

"Because I feel like it," the old lady replied, tartly.

As she struggled to wrest the axe out of the chopping block where it had imbedded itself deeply, I padded over and grabbed the sleeve of her right arm, tugging gently but firmly.

She frowned at me. "What are you doing, you fool dog? Let go of me."

Despite her protests, she allowed me to lead her away from the chopping block and the scattered chunks of firewood. Meredith shook her head, but before she could say anything more, the crunch of a vehicle's tires sounded on the gravel road in front of the house.

Abigail's wrinkled face twisted with dread. "Good lord, they're here!" she exclaimed.

I trotted eagerly ahead of the two women, anxious for my first glimpse of the dreaded nephew and his harpy wife.

A fancy red Lexus coupe pulled into Abigail's driveway at a fast clip and braked to a screeching halt just before it would have plowed into the steps leading up to the porch. Pine needles and gravel sprayed to either side of the tires. Behind me, I heard Abigail mutter a very unladylike expletive.

The driver's side of the Lexus sprang open and a man I presumed to be Caleb Tunner jumped out. I had a quick impression of a short, skinny man with dark thinning hair combed sideways over his head and a tight paunch jutting out over his belt before he raced over to Abigail and grabbed her in a bear hug.

"Aunt Abby!" he cried, lifting her off her feet and swinging her around in a circle.

Horrified shock registered on her face as she vainly tried to beat at his back with her pinned arms. "Put me down, you oaf!"

Reluctantly he did so, keeping his hands on her thin shoulders and grinning hugely, seemingly oblivious to the animosity that seethed on her lined face and in her narrowed eyes. "Aunt Abby, it's so good to see you again. It's been way too long."

"Speak for yourself, Caleb," Abigail replied.

The foolish grin on the man's face slipped for just a second and then returned in full force. "Ha! Dear Aunt Abby, I remember you always did have a dry sense of humor. You haven't changed a bit in all these years. When *was* the last time we saw each other, anyway? It seems like forever."

The old woman's lips tightened. "Believe me, forever's not long enough."

Caleb looked uncertain for a moment and I felt sorry for the poor man, facing the implacable animosity of his aunt. Thinking he could use a friendly gesture right about then, I wriggled myself in between him and Abigail, wagging my tail and grinning up at him. He gave me an irritated glance and pushed me rudely away with a sharp jab in the ribs from his bony knee.

"Get lost, you miserable mutt!"

Now I was not exactly a wimpy canine. After all, you have to be pretty tough to be a good detective, but that jab hurt and I let out an involuntary whimper, as much from shock at the harsh treatment as pain. No one had ever treated me so roughly before.

Quick anger flared across Meredith's face and her eyes narrowed dangerously. "Don't you dare touch my dog like that again."

If there was one thing my human was extremely passionate about, it was the prevention of cruelty to animals, especially me. She was like a ferocious mother bear protecting her cubs if she thought someone was ill-treating an animal.

Caleb Tunner barely glanced at her, an impatient scowl on his face. "I don't like dogs. Keep it away from me."

Meredith's lips tightened and she called me to her. I went gladly, my side still smarting from the sharp jab.

I no longer felt sorry for the man. I had been willing to give him a chance to disprove Abigail's unkind assessment of him, but as far as I was concerned at that moment, Caleb Tunner deserved every derogatory insult and verbal abuse that Abigail's cutting tongue was capable of dishing out. For a brief moment, I even contemplated reversing my decision not to bite him.

By now, a woman had climbed out of the passenger side of the car and was headed our way with a decidedly reluctant gait. I perked up a little, momentarily forgetting the callous treatment of Caleb and wondering if Abigail's description of her nephew's wife would be anywhere near the real thing.

Rowena Tunner drew up a few feet away from us. Her muddy brown eyes flicked to the log house and then to Abigail with barely concealed distaste. Unlike her husband, she made no move whatsoever to touch the old woman, either with a hug or a handshake.

"Hello, Abigail," she said, her mouth pinched into a thin line.

Rowena was taller than her husband and had hair the color and texture of yellow straw. She wore it in a frizzy knot on the top of her head and I thought—a little unkindly, to be sure—that if a bone had been thrust through the tangled tresses, she would have looked remarkably like a cavewoman. Except that cavewomen, as far as I knew, didn't wear tons of makeup and bright red lipstick.

My eyes flicked from Rowena to Caleb to Abigail, seeing the three of them frozen in a tableau that radiated iciness every bit as cutting as an arctic wind, while Meredith and I stood uncomfortably off to one side.

Abigail had been right. There was something decidedly fishy about this visit by Caleb and Rowena. Caleb's exuberant greeting of his aunt seemed to me as phony as a three-dollar bill and Rowena's cold aloofness was unmistakable.

I wondered what could possibly have brought the two of them up here from the big city of Toronto to Northern Ontario to visit an old woman whom they seemed to dislike as much as she did them.

Aha! I thought, eagerly. *Another case for Flint and Steele!*

Chapter 3

Abigail's nephew and his wife seemed none too pleased to discover that Meredith and I had been invited for supper.

With a glower aimed at us, Caleb said pointedly, "We haven't seen you for so long, Aunt Abby. There's a lot I'd like to talk to you about, and I'm sure Ms. Steele wouldn't be interested in hearing about our *private* family matters."

Meredith spoke up quickly. "Maybe Flint and I should leave you to your guests, Abby. We can visit some other time."

Abigail threw her a thunderous look. "Nonsense, Meredith," she said, through gritted teeth. "I *insist* you stay for supper."

Meredith sighed faintly, knowing it would be futile to protest further. I wondered if a well-placed nip on Caleb Tunner's skinny backside would provide us with a good enough excuse to avoid supper with the ill-mannered lout.

When Abigail called me up the porch steps and held the screen door open for me to enter the house, Caleb's thin, pale face darkened.

"That animal's not coming inside with us, is it?" he asked.

Abigail turned to him, hazel eyes widened in feigned surprise. "Well, of course he is. Flint is almost like a member of the family, aren't you, fella?"

She reached to scratch my ears and I stared at her in unfeigned surprise. For her to openly fuss over me like that with other people around, I knew the old lady's determination to aggravate her nephew at all costs must have been fierce indeed.

Caleb opened his mouth to say something further, but his wife stepped in with an impatient sigh. "Oh, for God's sakes, Caleb, it's only a dog! Stop making such a fuss. After all, it is *her* house."

"Damn right it is!" Abigail said, loudly.

Caleb glared at Rowena and she raised her plucked eyebrows in a meaningful manner, tilting her head slightly as though sending him a message.

After a moment, he growled, "Fine! Just keep that mutt away from me. I don't like dogs."

"Don't worry. Flint is smart enough to avoid people *he* doesn't like," Meredith assured him, sweetly.

Caleb gave her a dirty look.

Beside me, Abigail let out a hoarse chuckle. "Well, don't just stand there, you three. Come on into the house. I ain't serving you supper out here in the yard."

Like some kind of doggy dignitary, I found myself preceding everyone else into the house. Even though I knew it was only because Abigail wanted to annoy her nephew, I still couldn't help feeling rather smug at the preferential treatment.

Even though I loved the little log house that Meredith and I called home, I enjoyed visiting Abigail's house, too.

During the week, when Meredith was gone to her job as a sales analyst at the Ontario Lottery Corporation in the city, I often ambled over to Abigail's house and spent the day there. It was a little faded and worn and old-fashioned in places, but that was what gave it its particular charm. Abigail had made some concessions to modern technology, namely electricity and indoor plumbing, but many of the original furnishings and features her grandparents put into the house had been retained.

The living room and kitchen were my two favorite places. The most outstanding feature of the living room was the huge stone fireplace. Albert and Martha Tunner had collected the round stones used in the construction of the fireplace from along the shores of Lake Superior and had built the mantelpiece from a six-inch thick slab of highly polished oak.

A Navajo rug partially covered the wide wooden planks of the living room floor, its vibrant colors muted somewhat by time, but its beauty still apparent. Sitting on it in a semi-circle in front of the fireplace were a dark green sofa with a brown and orange crocheted afghan draped over the back, a comfortable tan-colored armchair that was just perfect for a dog to curl up in, and a burgundy rocker-recliner that was Abigail's favorite chair. Pine bookshelves, handmade by Albert Tunner over fifty years ago, lined both sides of the fireplace and were crammed full of books.

A set of curved wooden steps to the left of the fireplace led to the second floor where Abigail's bedroom occupied one whole side of the house and overlooked Whitefish Bay. On the other side of the narrow hallway, there was a smaller bedroom and a bathroom paneled in cedar.

The kitchen was big and homey. Abigail still used an old-fashioned, wood-burning cook stove with an oven for all her baking and cooking. The large table in the center of the kitchen was made from pine, nicked and scratched and dulled over the years by constant use. Cupboards with pine and glass doors held an assortment of mismatched dishes and handmade pottery mugs, as well as jars of preserves and other food items. Faded and worn braided rag rugs, handmade by Abigail's grandmother, Martha, were placed in front of the stove, the stainless steel sink and the door to the outside. The kitchen always seemed to carry the aroma of freshly baked bread, spicy tomato sauce or roasted meat. That was probably why it was one of my favorite places in the house.

That night, however, the aromas wafting from the kitchen made my sensitive nose twitch in alarm. I could smell chicken, but also an underlying odor of burnt meat and scorched potatoes.

Oh, oh! I thought, uneasily. From first-hand experience, I knew Abigail was an excellent cook. She very seldom burned anything, so this unusual smell was definitely an ominous sign of things to come during supper.

Caleb and Rowena seemed immune to the charms of Abigail's rustic log home. They looked around with barely-concealed aversion and contempt, standing stiffly in the middle of the living room as though afraid to touch anything. Rowena's bright, flowery silk dress and fashionable white sandals seemed somehow out-of-place amid the simple, countrified furnishings of the house. Caleb's expensive sports jacket, beige chino pants and highly polished leather shoes made him look like a model for GQ Magazine who had suddenly found himself plunked down in the middle of a Marlboro Country ad.

A mosquito that had followed us in from outside buzzed insistently around Rowena's frizzy topknot and she swatted at it futilely. "Ugh! I can't stand bugs!" she complained.

"Well, you'd better get used to them, girlie," Abigail said, unsympathetically. "We've got mosquitoes here big enough to carry off a squirrel and deer flies that'll take chunks of meat out of your hide."

Rowena inhaled sharply. The younger woman obviously wanted to make some cutting remark in response to Abigail's mockery, but instead she clamped her blood red lips tightly shut, looking like she had just bitten down on something sour.

I found it extremely interesting that both she and Caleb seemed to be harboring an almost overwhelming urge to throttle the disagreeable old woman, and yet were forcing themselves to quell the desire to do so.

Why were they so willing to put up with a seventy-five year old tyrant for a week in a place they obviously considered way beneath them? Maybe Meredith was right and they wanted to mend fences with Abigail before the old woman died. But somehow, I doubted it. And even if that was the reason, my detective instincts told me it would not be in the hopes of restoring familial love. More likely, they hoped to weasel a way into Abigail's will, although how they thought they could accomplish such a monumental task in only a week was beyond me.

I saw Abigail eyeing her nephew and his wife with a speculative glint and surmised that she was probably thinking along the same lines herself. If Caleb and Rowena Tunner thought they could win crafty old Abigail over in such a short period of time, they obviously did not know her at all.

If I had not already decided that I disliked the two of them immensely, I might have felt some sympathy for their upcoming battle with the old lady.

Chapter 4

Just as I feared, supper turned out to be a disaster. Abigail's pan-fried chicken breasts resembled chunks of blackened shoe leather and the potatoes had been boiled until they were soft and mushy and scorched in places. The green salad, consisting of nothing more than several leaves of lettuce and a few meager scrapings of carrot, was limp and wilted. Dessert turned out to be a bland rice pudding.

Caleb and Rowena gamely plowed through the unappetizing meal, although it was quite obvious they would rather have starved to death than eat it. Abigail sat there the whole time with a faint, self-satisfied smile on her face. She even made a point of throwing me tidbits of chicken every now and then, earning a glare from her nephew but no reproachful comments. I forced myself to choke down the unappetizing morsels just to annoy him.

At last, the excruciating ordeal ended and Caleb quickly pushed back from the table with a visibly relieved look. "Well, Aunt Abby, thank you for the meal. It was..."

"Awful, I know." Abigail finished the sentence for him; her face drooped in lines of unconvincing apology. "I'm just such a lousy cook. I'm sorry I couldn't have served you a better supper."

Meredith nearly choked on her rice pudding and had to take a quick drink from her glass of water. From my place on the floor beside her chair, I raised my eyes to Abigail's guileless face and whined in disbelief. I swore she could read my thoughts because she gave me a quick wink and twitched her lips in a faint smile.

Caleb and Rowena looked as though they wanted to agree wholeheartedly with Abigail's assessment of the meal, but instead, they murmured vague compliments that no one took seriously. Everyone knew the meal had been a disaster, but neither Caleb nor Rowena seemed willing to antagonize Abigail by complaining.

The old lady stood up, saying briskly, "Okay, you two, why don't you go bring your luggage in while Meredith and I clean up here, unless, of course, you've changed your mind and want to head back to Toronto? I can't say that I'd blame you, what with having to put up with my terrible cooking and all."

"Don't be silly, Aunt Abby," Caleb said, with a forced cheerfulness. "We wouldn't think of leaving just yet when we've hardly had a chance to visit."

He pretended not to notice her crestfallen expression and ushered Rowena hastily out of the kitchen, both of them obviously only too glad to escape the scene of the gastric crime.

As Meredith carried dishes over to the sink, Abigail leaned toward her and spoke in a low, conspiratorial whisper. "Well, what do you think? I figure if I continue to feed them unpalatable food, they just might turn around and skedaddle back to Toronto in no time flat."

Meredith grimaced. "Well, I can tell you, *I* certainly would be discouraged from staying if I knew I could look forward to such cuisine for the next week!"

Abigail chuckled. "I'm sure Her Highness is used to caviar and lobster, so I'm hoping my bland, overcooked food will scare her off."

Meredith shook her head. "Abigail Tunner, you are a wicked woman."

For a moment, the old lady's face lost its mischievous expression and turned cold and hard. "They're up to something, Meredith, and I don't intend to encourage whatever lame-brained scheme they have in mind. I'm sure they think I'm a feeble-minded, crazy old woman who will do whatever they ask if they butter me up enough. Well, they can just think again. If they want to play games, so can I and I have a lot more experience at being devious than they have."

"Okay," Meredith said, soothingly. "But please don't invite me over for any more meals while they're here, okay? I don't think my stomach could handle it."

Abigail grinned. "Wimp!" She looked at me. "You'll come back for another meal, won't you, Flint? I'm sure Caleb would love to have you drool at his feet while he's eating."

I gave her a pained look. First of all, I didn't drool. Well, okay, maybe a little bit, but only when it was really hot out. And secondly, my sentiments exactly matched Meredith's. After experiencing Abigail's good cooking for so long, the thought of eating more of what we had tonight did not appeal to me in the slightest.

"Even Flint has discriminating tastes," Meredith said, coming to my rescue and echoing my thoughts. "Besides, you know I don't condone cruelty to animals."

Abigail grunted. "Well, at least give me some ideas for unappetizing dishes I can serve to those two."

Still feeling insulted by the drooling comment, I padded out of the kitchen and into the living room, leaving the two women alone with their dishes and their culinary conspiracies.

Through the screen door, I could see Caleb ponderously climbing the porch steps, lugging an enormous suede suitcase that looked as though it weighed a ton. He puffed and panted as the expensive looking suitcase bumped roughly against the wooden planks of the steps.

"...put up with the old bag until then," he was saying as he approached the door.

Following on his heels and carrying what looked like a small cosmetics bag and nothing else, Rowena hissed, "Not so loud, Caleb! She might hear. And for God's sakes, quit banging that suitcase around like that! You know how much it cost."

He glared at her over his shoulder. "Why don't you try carrying it if you think it's so easy?" He squinted through the screen door into the living room and saw me standing in front of the sofa, my head cocked curiously. "Besides, there's only that mangy mutt to hear what we say."

Mangy mutt? I couldn't help myself. My lip curled in a snarl and a low growl rumbled out of my mouth as I stared at him through the screen door. It seemed as though every time Caleb Tunner opened his mouth, he gave me more reason to dislike him.

Having made my feelings known, I then deliberately jumped on the tan armchair and turned around three times before settling down with my chin on my paws, my eyes glaring disdainfully at Caleb.

As he struggled with the door and the heavy suitcase, the disagreeable man looked daggers at me.

"God, remind me never to sit in that chair!" he groused to his wife. "It's probably infested with fleas."

Rowena shuddered slightly. "Ugh! Don't even mention bugs! I don't know how I'm going to stand this place for a week. Are you sure there isn't some other way?"

Caleb deposited the enormous suede suitcase by the staircase and inclined his head toward the kitchen where the hum of voices and the splashing of water could be heard.

"We've already been through this a hundred times, Rowena," he growled in a low voice. "It'll work out, you wait and see. Meanwhile, we'll just have to put up with all of this until then. Who knows? With any luck, we won't have to stay the whole week."

He pointed at me in the armchair. "Get down off the furniture, Fido," he commanded.

I merely raised my head and stared at him, silently lifting my lips over my teeth. He backed off, his face glistening with sweat and irritation.

"I'll get the rest of the luggage," he muttered, stomping to the door and letting it bang shut loudly behind him.

When he was gone, Rowena shot a sneaky look toward the kitchen and then tiptoed over to the fireplace. She began running her hands over the round stones, pushing and prodding them and the concrete in between, unaware of my keen interest.

Curious, I watched her from the vantage point of the armchair. What did she hope to find? Buried treasure stashed behind a secret removable stone? As far as I knew, every stone was still as solidly embedded in the concrete as it had been on the day old Albert Tunner built the fireplace. But on the other hand, it wouldn't have surprised me in the slightest to discover that there were indeed secret caches of valuables hidden somewhere among those stones. Old Albert had been a bit of an eccentric and might very well have stashed jewels or money in the fireplace rather than trust them to a bank. And Abigail herself was certainly unconventional enough to have thought of the idea as well.

Just then, Caleb clattered up the porch steps with two more large pieces of luggage and Rowena jumped guiltily, moving quickly away from the fireplace. Her thin shoulders slumped in relief when she realized it was only her husband.

Abigail and Meredith came into the living room at the same moment that Caleb awkwardly wrestled the screen door open.

"Ah, I see you've brought your luggage in," Abigail said. "Why don't you bring it upstairs and I'll show you to your room."

Caleb's face glowed pink from exertion. "I could use a hand. There's still another suitcase out in the car."

Abigail's gray eyebrows rose slightly. "There's more?"

Rowena lifted her chin and glared haughtily down her nose. "Well, of course. After all, we *are* going to be here for a week."

"Of course," Abigail said, expressionlessly. She turned to the staircase and started up the curved wooden steps. "Well, come along, Caleb. You might as well carry those up now while you still have the energy."

Caleb shot a murderous look at his aunt's back and then began to trudge up the stairs with the two heavy suitcases. Rowena picked up the small case she had placed on the sofa, and skirting the huge suede suitcase as though it was a dangerous beast of some kind, followed her puffing husband up the staircase, her high-heeled sandals clattering loudly on the uncarpeted steps.

From below, Meredith and I watched the three people until they disappeared from sight. Then my partner shook her head and looked at me, eyes glinting with amusement.

"Come on, Flint. That's our cue to leave. Let's get out of here while we can!"

Chapter 5

The next day was Monday and Meredith had to drive into the city to work. Before she left, she gave me a piece of sage advice. "If I were you, I'd stay away from Abigail's today, Flint. We don't need that nephew of hers chasing you off the property with her old shotgun."

I assumed my most innocent, guileless expression, which I didn't think she entirely believed because she gave me a skeptical look before getting into the vehicle and driving off.

As soon as the silver Kia Rondo disappeared around the first bend of the gravel road, I took off like a shot for Abigail's house. Before going directly there, though, I made a quick detour over to Geordie's place. I thought maybe the young scamp might like to help me stake out Abigail's house and keep an eye on her nephew and his wife. Surveillance could be pretty dull and boring at times and having company might make the hours go faster.

When I reached the Ford house, however, there was no sign of Geordie, and then I remembered Linda was taking him to the vet to get his annual shots that day. I shuddered slightly in sympathy for my little buddy's upcoming ordeal. Fortunately for me, my own trip to the vet had taken place earlier in the spring, but the unpleasant memories still lingered in the back of my mind.

Poor little guy, I thought, as I lifted my leg by the front steps and left him a pee-mail, telling him to meet me at Abigail's place when he got back from the city.

I raced back toward the log house, eager to see if Caleb and Rowena had survived the night with Abigail. Maybe they were already on their way back to Toronto, having decided that the pain and agony of putting up with the old lady's caustic tongue and overt hostility was not worth whatever they had come there for.

Just before I reached Abigail's place, a rabbit bounded across the gravel road in front of me, and almost without conscious thought, I swerved after it, excitement and anticipation thrumming through my body. Several meters into the thick brush on the side of the road, I suddenly skidded to a halt, realizing how close the enticing scent of bunny had come to distracting me from the mission at hand. I watched in some disappointment as the soft brown rump of the rabbit disappeared under a fallen log.

With a faint huff of regret, I trotted back to the road and continued on toward Abigail's house. Luckily, I had overcome the temptation of a good chase through the bush, although I wondered if it might have been more exciting than what awaited me at Abigail's.

As I neared the last bend before the log house, I heard raised voices and decided to continue on through the underbrush at the side of the road to avoid being seen. I wanted to carry out my surveillance covertly without Caleb and Rowena being aware of my presence.

Long before I saw her, I heard Abigail's querulous voice coming from the roofed porch at the front of the house. Peeking out from under several low hanging balsam fir boughs at the end of the driveway, I watched as the old woman clomped down the steps followed closely by Rowena and Caleb.

Abigail tried to turn around several times, but the two people behind her relentlessly pushed forward, forcing her to continue on down to the foot of the steps.

"I don't feel like going into town!" Abigail said, stubbornly. "I want to stay right here."

"Now, Aunt Abby, a change of scenery will be good for you," Caleb said, his voice dripping with false cheerfulness. "You and Rowena can spend some quality girl-time shopping together."

Almost identical expressions of disgust twisted the faces of both Abigail and Rowena in front of him. Neither woman seemed particularly thrilled by the prospect.

"Sure," Rowena said, turning to glare sourly at her husband. "I really need some things and I don't know your little town, Abigail, so I'd appreciate it if you would come with me to show me where to shop."

"What *things* could you possibly need?" Abigail demanded. "You brought fifty pieces of luggage with you, for heaven's sakes. If you didn't pack something, then do without it."

Caleb gave a high-pitched, almost girlish laugh and cupped his hand around the old woman's elbow, leading her firmly toward the red Lexus. "Dear Aunt Abby, that wonderful sense of humor of yours! Now, don't be so difficult. You and Rowena go into the city and have a wonderful time. Don't worry about me. I'm just going to stay here and relax after that long drive yesterday."

He opened the passenger door and practically shoved Abigail into the front seat, then stood with his hand on the top of the door after closing it as if afraid the old lady

32

would jump back out before Rowena had a chance to climb into the driver's seat. From my place of concealment at the end of the driveway, I couldn't see Abigail's face, but the rigid set of her gray head told me that she was not at all pleased with the idea of a trip into Sault Ste. Marie with her nephew's wife.

I jumped backward as Rowena reversed quickly out of the driveway, spraying gravel and pine needles in every direction. I caught just a glimpse of Abigail's rebellious face before the Lexus took off at a speed more suitable to a six-lane highway than a narrow, curving gravel road.

As soon as the car was out of sight, Caleb blew out his breath in a gusty sigh and wiped his forehead. Errant strands of long hair combed over his balding head flipped sideways in a slight breeze, giving him a lopsided look. Absently, he brushed them back over his head but they immediately flipped the other way again.

"Well, thank God, that's done!" he said, out loud. "Poor Rowena. I don't envy her having to put up with that old bag, but better her than me."

Smiling a bit maliciously, he turned and started up the steps.

I slunk out from behind the balsam fir and stalked closer to the house, keeping to the side of the road in case Caleb turned and I had to duck back into hiding in a hurry.

He entered the house, letting the screen door slam shut loudly behind him. I trotted as quietly as I could up the porch steps and peeked cautiously through the screen. Caleb stood by the end table near Abigail's rocker recliner holding the telephone receiver to his ear. I struggled to hear his end of the conversation since he had his back to me and his voice was slightly muffled.

"Okay, the coast is clear. I got the old lady out of the house, but I don't know for how long." His voice rose nervously. "I know, I know! But she's as crazy as a loon, and there's no telling what she might do to get away from

Rowena and back out here. So, you'd better hurry up." I saw him run his hand nervously across his thinning scalp. "No, no, of course I'm not giving you orders. I'm just trying to tell you there's not a lot of time to lose. It's about twenty-five kilometers from the city to here. Just keep going on Second Line West past the airport turnoff until you see the sign for Gros Cap at the bottom of a hill and a paved road called Douglas Drive. Abigail's road is the second one to the left past Douglas. Follow it until you come to a fork and then take the left hand side. You can't miss her driveway. There's a pole by the side of it with a bunch of weird faces on it."

The pole with the weird faces was actually a small totem pole carved and given to Abigail by Damien Nadeau, a First Nations fisherman who had a commercial fishing boat on Lake Superior and who often supplied the old lady with fresh whitefish and lake trout. Caleb's total lack of knowledge about totem poles didn't surprise me in the least. Even though Abigail claimed her family was descended from the Ojibwa, her citified nephew probably had no inkling whatsoever of First Nations traditions or customs.

Quelling my disdain with some difficulty, I turned my attention back to his end of the conversation.

"Yeah, yeah, I'm sure. No, of course I wouldn't deliberately bring you out here on a wild-goose chase. It's definitely here. Yeah, okay, see you in about half an hour."

He put down the phone, fumbling the receiver a bit in its cradle. I ducked away from the door as he turned around, but not before I saw him swipe at beads of sweat running down his face and heard him mumble, "God, I sure hope like hell it's here!"

Scooting back down the steps, I hid behind a wild-rose bush to the right of the porch where I laid down in the shade to contemplate what I'd just heard. It sounded like Caleb and Rowena were in cahoots with someone in their scheme, whatever it was, and that someone was now on his or her way out here.

I laid my chin on my paws, prepared to wait for the arrival of the mysterious accomplice. Meanwhile, Caleb remained in the house and I itched to know what he was up to in there. But even though I had mastered the trick of opening the screen door on my own, I knew I wouldn't be able to do it quietly enough without Caleb hearing. So rather than risk having the unpleasant man discover my presence and chase me off with Abigail's old shotgun, I decided to wait behind the rose bush until the other person arrived. There might be an opportunity later for me to sneak into the house and find out what the two of them were up to.

I must have dozed off for a few moments, because the next thing I knew, something poked me in the backside and I jumped up with a startled growl. Whirling around and expecting to see Caleb grinning murderously as he pointed the shotgun at me, I saw instead the inquisitive, friendly face of my little buddy, Geordie. He had returned from the city, thankfully still in one piece from his visit to the vet, and had read my pee-mail by the front steps of his house. Even though he was pretty useless at detective work most of the time, I was still pleased to see him. As I said, surveillance could sometimes be lonely work and I figured keeping me company while I kept an eye on Caleb should be well within Geordie's capabilities. That was, as long as a squirrel or chipmunk didn't decide to make a sudden appearance to distract him.

I listened with half an ear while Geordie related his scary visit to the vet. It had taken the better part of the drive back from the city before the poor little mutt had been able to stop his nervous trembling. Although I sympathized with my buddy's distressful experience, most of my attention remained riveted on Abigail's house where I was sure her nephew was up to no good.

A few minutes later, I heard the sound of tires crunching on the gravel road and a black SUV with tinted windows came into view. It pulled into the driveway and I sat up quickly, hushing Geordie's excited voice. For once, the little scamp listened to me, his white face with the black eye patches alight with avid curiosity.

The driver's door of the SUV opened and a big man with a cigarette dangling from his mouth stepped out. He was wearing a black leather jacket despite the sultry heat of the July morning and stood looking around with wary caution. His face was ugly and pockmarked, and his large meaty hands were the size of baseball mitts. Despite his formidable bulk, however, he moved with the peculiar grace of a boxer, his expensive shoes barely making a whisper as he crossed the gravel to the front yard. He tossed the still burning cigarette butt off to one side and it landed just in front of the bush where Geordie and I hid. Wrinkling my nose at the acrid odor of cigarette smoke, I resisted the urge to sneeze, hoping the stranger wouldn't glance toward the bush and see two pairs of bright inquisitive eyes peering out from behind it.

Before the man reached the bottom of the steps, a slightly disheveled Caleb appeared at the screen door, his narrow face pinched in a tense expression.

He opened the door, gesturing quickly. "Biggs, good, you're here! Hurry up and come inside. I don't know how much longer Rowena is going to be able to keep the old woman in the city. She called me from her cell phone a few minutes ago and said that Abigail is creating horrible scenes in all the stores, demanding that Rowena drive her back home."

The big man named Biggs gazed up at him from the bottom of the steps with a bland, inscrutable expression. "Well, you'd better hope that wife of yours can keep the old woman away for as long as necessary, Tunner. If she comes back too soon, it won't be healthy for her." His voice was gravelly and rough, as devoid of expression as his fleshy face.

Caleb's face blanched slightly. "You said no one would get hurt! That was part of the deal. God knows I can't stand the old biddy, but that doesn't mean I want to see her hurt."

Biggs stared at him, his ugly face unmoved. "Then, we'd better get a move on, hadn't we? Mr. Connelly doesn't like to be kept waiting."

At the mention of the name, Caleb's face paled even further and he nodded quickly, standing aside as the big man brushed past him into the house.

I exchanged a startled glance with Geordie. All of my detective instincts flared to high alert as the ominous words of the two men replayed in my mind.

What was Caleb Tunner up to? And what did he mean by Abigail possibly getting hurt?

Chapter 6

From our hiding place behind the rose bush, Geordie and I could hear curious noises coming from inside the house. From the scrapes and thumps and thuds, it almost sounded as though the furniture was being moved around.

Despite the danger of being spotted, I couldn't sit still behind the rose bush any longer. I had to see what was happening inside. Telling Geordie to stay put behind the bush, I slunk up the steps of the porch and resumed my cautious surveillance through the screen door.

The big man named Biggs was effortlessly holding one end of the sofa high up in the air while Caleb poked and prodded quickly at the underside. He shook his head and the big man dropped the sofa to the floor with a loud thump.

"Not here," Caleb said, his voice tinged with worry.

Biggs glared at him, a dark expression beginning to tighten the features of his pockmarked face. "You'd better be right about this, Tunner. Mr. Connelly won't be too pleased if I go back to Toronto empty-handed."

Caleb shook his head quickly. "It's here somewhere, I know it is. I thought for sure it was hidden under the mattress like she said, but I already checked there so it's got to be somewhere else. The old lady is as crazy as a bedbug, so I wouldn't doubt she hid it in a crazy place."

Biggs looked at the big stone fireplace. "What about there?"

"Rowena did a quick search yesterday and couldn't find anything. But she didn't have a chance to look too closely. We can check there again in case she missed something."

The two men strode to the fireplace and began pushing and prodding at the stones and concrete much as Rowena had done the day before. Caleb stuck his head and right arm up inside the dark depths of the chimney and was rewarded for his efforts by a shower of black soot that rained down on his upturned face. He spluttered and coughed and withdrew quickly, looking remarkably like a chimney sweep, and I had to suppress a small snigger of amusement at the lout's discomfort. It served him right for his violation of Abigail's home and, *ahem*, hospitality.

Biggs grunted and a grimace that possibly passed for a smile twisted his thick lips. "Careful you don't get those fancy clothes of yours too dirty, Tunner. It's going to be hard to replace them in your current financial situation."

Caleb's soot-stained face flushed, but he didn't say anything.

At that moment, the telephone beside Abigail's recliner jangled shrilly and Caleb screamed and jumped; the startled whites of his eyes bugged out from the blackness of his face. He clutched at his chest for a moment, panting slightly, and then grabbed the receiver, cutting off the second ring in mid-jangle. "Yeah?"

Under the black soot stains, his face twisted with frustration as he listened. Even from as far away as I was, I could faintly hear the shrill voice on the other end.

"Okay, okay, calm down. No, we haven't found it yet, but we still have some time to look. Try to drive back as slowly as you can without giving the old bag a chance to jump out of the car. Yeah, yeah, I know it would be great if she did that, but we don't need to explain to the police why she jumped out and why you ran her over. Just stall for as long as possible. We'll keep looking, but so far we haven't had much luck."

His eyes darted toward Biggs as he said this and his Adam's apple bobbed in an agitated gulp when the big man lowered his head and glowered like a bull about to charge.

Caleb replaced the receiver and said unnecessarily, "They're on their way back. Rowena can't keep the old lady in the city any longer, short of tying her up and gagging her. Much as that would be a godsend, I don't think it's an option we can take advantage of right now." He glanced at the expensive watch on his left wrist. "We've probably got about another half hour before they get here. But maybe you should go now, Biggs. You really don't need to be here to help with this, anyway. Rowena and I can handle it."

Biggs grunted sourly. "Yeah, yeah, just like you handled your gambling debts. Mr. Connelly sent me here because he doesn't trust you, Tunner, and neither do I. Now stop wasting time and let's get on with it."

Caleb nodded jerkily. "Okay, whatever you say. I think we've pretty well covered this room. Let's check out the kitchen next."

The two men proceeded toward the kitchen and I trotted silently back down the steps to where Geordie waited behind the bush. He was full of questions, but I quickly hushed him and led the way back down the driveway, using the black SUV to shield our getaway.

By now, I had a pretty good idea of what Caleb and Rowena and the mysterious Biggs were up to. It seemed very likely that Caleb had gotten in over his head with gambling debts and now owed a great deal of money to Biggs' boss, Mr. Connelly. For some reason, Caleb thought Abigail had a bunch of money or jewels stashed somewhere in her house and he was hoping to find it in order to pay off his debts. That was the whole purpose of this sudden visit to an aunt he hadn't seen in years and for whom he obviously felt no love or affection.

I growled at the sheer audacity of the man. How dare he come here, hoping to steal money from Abigail and disrupting her life because of his greed and stupidity!

At that moment, a rabbit hopped out of the underbrush in front of us and high-tailed it across the road into the bush on the other side. I was almost positive it was the same bunny I had spotted on the way over to Abigail's house earlier that morning, coming back to deliberately tease and taunt me. But this time I welcomed the distraction; it was just what I needed to get rid of some of the anger and frustration I was feeling toward Caleb Tunner.

With Geordie yapping excitedly by my side, the two of us merrily chased after the bunny, dodging in and out between trees and shrubs and over fallen logs and rocks. The pursuit was invigorating and exciting, even though the wily rabbit eluded us at every turn. Finally, we lost sight of it completely, and Geordie howled in disappointment. I, on the other hand, was not bothered by the outcome. The thrilling chase had served its purpose by momentarily distracting me from the wicked, primal urge to inflict some serious damage on Caleb's skinny backside with my canines.

Geordie and I trotted down to the shore, our tongues hanging down to our knees, and waded into the cool water to relieve our heated bodies. After a refreshing swim, Geordie headed home and I plopped down in the shade of a big oak tree by the fork in the road, keeping an eye out for the red Lexus.

Somehow, I had to let Abigail know about the deceitful plans of her nephew and his wife, although the old woman was not stupid by any means. She was already plenty suspicious of their motives, and I didn't think it would take too long for her to fully understand their underhanded intentions.

I lifted my head at the sound of a vehicle coming from behind me. In the next moment, the black SUV barreled around the corner and raced by the oak tree where I lay in the shade. At the same time, I caught the flash of a red vehicle through the trees coming in the opposite direction, also at a high rate of speed. I jumped to my feet, terrified for a moment that the two vehicles would crash headfirst into each other on the narrow, winding stretch of road. Just when a collision seemed inevitable, Biggs cranked the steering wheel hard to the right to avoid the Lexus, and the back end of the SUV fishtailed slightly, narrowly missing the trees lining the road. He barely even slowed down as he roared past and kept on going. I could see Abigail in the front seat of the Lexus, shaking her fist furiously at the disappearing SUV.

Rowena clutched the steering wheel in a death grip and stared straight ahead as the Lexus sped by me. Her face looked as black and furious as the violent thunderclouds that often boiled across the bay in late summer. I grinned, picturing the humiliation and agony Abigail must have put her through on their so-called quality girl-time shopping trip.

I raced up the road in the wake of the gravel storm kicked up by the speeding car, anxious to let Abigail know somehow that Caleb had been up to no good while she had been gone. I reached her house in time to see Rowena erupt out of the car and charge up the steps of the porch, her fashionable high heels clattering loudly on the wooden planks.

Caleb appeared at the screen door. I noticed his face looked freshly scrubbed and he had changed his shirt to get rid of the telltale soot stains. He jumped back quickly to avoid being trampled by his wife as she jostled by him and into the house.

"So, Rowena, dear, how did the shopping trip go?" he asked, acting as though the trip into the city had been a perfectly normal excursion.

Rowena sent him a venomous look that would have melted the polar ice cap in the Arctic, but Caleb pretended not to notice. He stood on the top step of the porch, looking down at Abigail as she struggled to extricate herself from the low-slung car.

"Did you and Rowena have a good time in the city, Aunt Abby?" he asked.

The old woman glared at him. "Oh, yeah, just peachy."

She finally succeeded in getting out of the car and slammed the door with somewhat unnecessary force. Caleb winced but refrained from saying anything, even though the effort obviously cost him a lot.

I trotted around the back of the Lexus and nudged Abigail's hand with my cold nose.

She jumped and gasped, a tiny frown between her eyes. "Good heavens, Flint, you startled me! What do you want, you silly dog?"

I took the sleeve of her shirt in my teeth and tugged, trying to drag her toward the rose bush by the porch. She shook her arm in an attempt to dislodge me, but I just clenched my teeth tighter in the fabric of her shirt.

"What in tarnation is wrong with you, dog?" she exclaimed.

Out of the corner of my eye, I could see Caleb standing at the top of the porch steps, his face twisted in a dark expression.

Finally, Abigail quit resisting and let me pull her along, although she continued to grumble and grouse the whole time. I led her to the rose bush and then let go of her sleeve, bending my head to poke at the cigarette butt lying on the ground by the porch steps and wrinkling my sensitive nose slightly at the unpleasant acrid odor.

Abigail had a strong aversion to smoking and didn't allow tobacco products of any kind anywhere on her property, so I knew the appearance of the butt would prompt a quick reaction out of her. And I was right.

"What's this?" she demanded, bending and picking up the offensive object. She held it gingerly between her fingertips as though afraid it was contaminated with some deadly poison.

Her eyes suddenly narrowed as she locked gazes with her nephew. "Caleb," she said, in a low, dangerous voice.

He appeared genuinely confused. "What?"

She waggled the butt between her fingers. "Were you smoking on my property while I was gone?"

Even though in this instance he was entirely innocent, the animosity in her voice made him blanch slightly and look guilty. "No, I don't smoke."

"Then how did this cigarette butt get here?"

"How should I know?"

Abigail's suspicious eyes narrowed even further. "Was someone else here?"

I wagged my tail furiously and whined. Abigail stared at me with an inquisitive lift of her left eyebrow, and I put on the most convincing expression I could to let her know she had hit the nail right on the head.

"No, nobody was here," Caleb said, lying through his teeth.

"What about that black vehicle that almost ran into your wife's fancy car? There are no other houses on this road except Meredith's and mine. And Meredith's not home. Are you telling me whoever was in that SUV didn't come here?"

Caleb frowned in apparent puzzlement. "Black vehicle? Oh, that guy. He was just somebody who was lost."

I growled at him and he snapped. "Shut up, dog! What are you doing here, anyway? Scat! Get back to your own house, you mangy mutt!"

"Leave Flint alone," Abigail said, crossly. "He's got more right to be here than you do."

She contemplated the distasteful object in her hand for a moment longer and then put it in the breast pocket of her plaid shirt. I watched with some trepidation, hoping she wouldn't throw it away later. It was a significant piece of evidence, but aside from what I'd already done, I couldn't think of any other way to impress upon her the meaning of its presence in her yard.

At times like this, I wished I could speak in a human tongue instead of dogese, or that humans could understand my language better. But, alas, we all had our limitations. All I could do was supply Abigail with clues as best I could and hope that her naturally suspicious nature and complete distrust of her nephew would lead her to the right conclusion.

Chapter 7

Meredith arrived home from work around four-thirty, tired and hot and ready for a nice glass of red wine. To my delight, she had picked up roasted chicken and potatoes for supper and we retired to the deck to enjoy our meal in the late afternoon sun.

With a contented sigh, Meredith sank down on to the cushioned swing and began to wiggle the toes of her bare foot up and down my back as I lay on the warm boards of the deck in front of her. I half-closed my eyes in ecstasy and rolled over so she could do the same to my belly. I couldn't help myself. Tough detective that I was, I was also a big softie when it came to pampering, especially from my favorite human.

"Boy, what a day!" Meredith said, blowing her breath out into a tired sigh and taking a sip of her red wine. "Mondays can be such a pain sometimes! Right, Flint? I'll bet you're glad this day is over, too. I can't imagine how bored you must be while I'm at work."

I gave her an upside-down droll look. How little did she know! I was bursting to tell her all about my *boring* day, but there were other priorities to be addressed first; namely, the box of fragrant chicken sitting on the small table by the swing. The tantalizing aroma was driving me crazy as I realized how much my adventures that day had whetted my appetite.

Meredith saw the direction of my upside-down eyes as they were drawn irresistibly toward the box of chicken, and she laughed. "I know that look! You're starving, aren't you, boy? I guess Abigail didn't slip you any tasty treats today, did she?"

I rolled quickly upright as she reached for a chicken breast, tore off a piece of the meat and tossed it to me. I made short work of it and waited expectantly for another.

As we ate the delicious chicken, Meredith gave another sigh and looked out over the calm waters of the bay, glinting like thousands of sparkling diamonds under the late afternoon sun. She swatted lazily at a buzzing mosquito. "This is much better than what we had for supper last night, isn't it, Flint? I wonder how poor Caleb and Rowena are doing with Abigail. I hope she hasn't poisoned them yet, although it wouldn't surprise me if she slipped a little strychnine into their overcooked string beans."

After witnessing the ominous interaction between that unpleasant man Biggs and Caleb Tunner earlier that morning, I wondered uneasily if maybe we should have been worrying about *Abigail* being poisoned by her nephew and his wife instead of the other way around.

Meredith chuckled and threw me another piece of chicken. "I think she's being a little too obvious in her methods, but it doesn't seem to be discouraging Caleb and Rowena from staying."

A tiny frown replaced the smile on her face. "I wonder why they came here. There's certainly no love lost between the three of them, but Caleb and Rowena seem determined for some reason to put up with Abigail's spite and insults at all costs. They must be hoping to get something out of this visit other than a sudden surge of love and affection from an old woman who'd sooner shoot them than hug them."

A look of worry crossed Meredith's face. "Well, whatever they're up to, I just hope Abigail doesn't get hurt by it."

Even though I knew she was probably thinking in terms of emotional pain rather than physical harm, I was glad to see she harbored the same doubts and misgivings that I did and that she wasn't just arbitrarily dismissing Abigail's suspicions as those of a crotchety old hermit who disliked everyone on general principle. Something unsavory was definitely happening at the Tunner homestead and it was up to Flint and Steele to discover what it was before someone got hurt.

After supper, Meredith and I set out on our evening walk, following the driveway up to Second Line West and then along a well-worn path that wove through stands of oak, maple and pine at the bottom of Marshall Hill just past Douglas Drive.

The scent of sun-warmed pine needles drifted past our noses. Mosquitoes buzzed lazily around us, but the sultry heat of the summer evening kept them from becoming too pesky.

Usually, I spent most of my time on these walks exploring the numerous enticing scents off to the sides of the trail, but my bunny adventure with Geordie earlier that afternoon had left me a little too tired to pursue my normal activities. I stayed close to Meredith, content just to amble along and enjoy the scenery.

The shaded trail meandered for a couple of kilometers before ending up at Shatruck Road where we turned around and headed back home. Just as we started down the gravel road toward our house, we heard a vehicle coming up behind us. It sounded like it was going at a fairly fast clip and Meredith turned. With a slight frown, she urged me further off to the side of the road to avoid being hit.

A black SUV sped toward us.

"Slow down, you idiot!" she hollered, anger coloring her voice.

My hackles rose instantly when I recognized the vehicle as the same one the unpleasant man named Biggs had been driving earlier that day. My detective instincts kicked into high gear. What was he doing back again?

To my great unease, the SUV pulled to a stop beside us and Biggs leaned out the window, another cigarette dangling from his thick lips. His ugly, pockmarked face seemed friendly enough, but his eyes were cold and hard. "Nice evening for a walk," he said, in his gravelly voice.

I placed myself protectively between Meredith and the SUV, the hair on my back standing straight up and a hostile growl rumbling through my quivering body.

Meredith placed a soothing hand on my head and murmured, "Easy, boy."

I continued to glare up at the ugly man in the vehicle, my throat vibrating constantly with the growl. Meredith shot me a curious glance, no doubt wondering why I was exhibiting such a negative reaction to the stranger. By nature, I was not an aggressive dog. On the contrary, I was quite sociable and more likely to lick someone to death with doggy kisses than to bite him or her. But whenever any of my human or canine friends were threatened or treated badly by unpleasant people like Biggs or Caleb and Rowena Tunner, I found myself reverting back to the protective, defensive instincts of my wild ancestors.

My unusually hostile behavior caused a wariness to settle over Meredith's pretty face and to my relief, she stepped back a pace from the SUV and the man leaning out the window. "Yes, it is a nice evening," she answered, politely.

The big man squinted at me. His thick lips twitched faintly and his eyebrow raised a fraction. "What's the matter with your dog? He doesn't seem very friendly."

Instead of assuring him that I was the friendliest pooch on the planet as she normally would, Meredith nodded tersely. "He's very protective of me, especially around strangers." She made it sound as though I would rip his head off in a second if he tried anything funny, and I curled my lips in an intimidating snarl to show him that I would be more than happy to do so if the need arose.

Unfortunately, my show of aggression had little effect on his type of gangster mentality. No doubt he faced much more intimidating threats in his line of work than a growling Labrador retriever with a cute face, which was how most humans described me. Regretfully, my benign appearance often made it difficult for me to convince people to take me seriously as a hard-nosed, no-nonsense detective. In this instance, Biggs merely looked at me with vague contempt and waved a hand as though dismissing the very notion that I could do him any harm.

"Pretty area," he said. "You live down this road? Does it end up at the lake?"

The question sounded innocent enough, but in my heightened state of agitation, I heard a menacing underlying note that convinced me there was more to it than just idle curiosity.

Meredith must have sensed it too because she said, "This is actually a private driveway. If you want to see the lake, there's a public boat launch further down Second Line and the street itself ends at a turnaround by the shore."

"Private driveway, eh? Many people live down this way?"

Her eyes narrowed slightly. "Why do you want to know?" she asked.

I could see that his questions were making her increasingly suspicious and wary, and I praised my human partner for her intelligence and perceptiveness. I didn't have to worry about her divulging too much information to Biggs. Although friendly and relatively trusting by nature, she was also much too smart to completely trust a stranger, especially one as menacing as Biggs.

He shrugged. "No particular reason, just curious. Never been down this way before, so I thought I'd check out the scenery."

I gnashed my teeth in frustration, wishing I could communicate to Meredith somehow that this man was a dangerous, lying gangster who, along with Abigail's repugnant nephew and his wife, posed a serious threat to Abigail.

"Well, enjoy your drive," Meredith said, making it clear she didn't intend to converse any further.

"Yeah, sure," Biggs said, and flicked his cigarette out the window.

It landed near Meredith's sandaled foot and her eyes narrowed with a flash of anger as she bent to retrieve it. "I think you dropped something," she said, coldly, holding the smoldering butt out to the man.

Like Abigail, Meredith had an affinity for the environment and hated to see it despoiled by unsightly litter. It angered both her and Abigail to no end when people came from the city and left their garbage and broken beer bottles lying around with little regard for their actions. More often than not, the residents of Gros Cap had to clean up the messes left behind by these inconsiderate slobs.

"One of these days, I'm going to follow one of those imbeciles home and dump a whole bag of garbage on their front step," Abigail often threatened. "See how *they* like it!"

Biggs gazed expressionlessly from the cigarette butt to Meredith's stony face. His cold eyes flickered slightly with scorn and he made no move to take the butt from her. Instead, he put the SUV in reverse and backed quickly down the road, the tires spinning slightly on the loose gravel.

Meredith stood looking after him, shaking her head. "Moron!" she said.

She ruffled my ears. "You didn't like him, either, did you, Flint? I don't blame you for growling at him. That guy gives me the creeps. I don't believe for one second that he's just out here for a drive. I think he's up to something."

She sighed and bent to stub out the glowing end of the cigarette butt before placing it in the pocket of her shorts. "Let's cut through the bush to get home," she suggested. "That man could be waiting down the road to see where we go. I don't trust him for one minute and I certainly don't want to lead him right to our front door."

I agreed wholeheartedly with her suggestion. Although I was pretty sure Biggs was just trying to get information out of her about how many people lived close to Abigail's house so he and the younger Tunners could search her property without being observed, I worried that the unsavory character could also cause trouble for *us* if we weren't careful.

Chapter 8

We arrived back at the house without spotting Biggs anywhere in the vicinity. I wanted to gnash my teeth in anger at the thought of that criminal sullying our little piece of paradise with his ugly presence.

Just as Meredith opened the door, the telephone rang and she hurried to answer it. She grimaced and held the receiver away from her ear as an irate voice boomed loudly out of the tiny speaker. I could clearly hear Abigail's wail on the other end. "I can't stand it any longer! I need to come over to your place before I do something drastic."

"Of course," Meredith said, rubbing her right ear as she transferred the phone to her left. "Come on over. Flint and I just got back from our walk."

"I warn you, though, I'm not in a very good mood," Abigail said, darkly.

Meredith grinned but kept her voice soothing as she said, "I'll make you a nice cup of tea."

"Tea!" the old woman snorted. "The way I feel, I need a whole bottle of rum to drown my sorrows!"

Meredith winced again when the receiver banged down in her ear.

She raised her eyebrows at me. The only alcohol Abigail ever drank was the occasional hot rum toddy when she had a cold in the winter. Otherwise, she abstained almost religiously from imbibing alcoholic beverages. Meredith even had a hard time convincing her to drink half a glass of champagne on New Year's Eve.

The situation must have been pretty desperate indeed at the Tunner homestead for Abigail to talk about breaking her long-standing tradition of non-drinking.

Five minutes later, the old woman arrived on our doorstep, fuming. Before Meredith even had a chance to fully open the door and say hello, Abigail charged past her into the living room, her face set in a black scowl.

"I'm going stark raving bonkers, girlie! That man and his wife are driving me crazy." She threw her hands into the air. "Why in heaven's name are they torturing me like this? What have I ever done to them?"

"Besides try to poison them, you mean?" Meredith asked.

"Hah! Serves them right for plunking themselves uninvited on my doorstep! What do they expect, lobster and caviar?" Her eyes suddenly lit up. "Wait a minute! I just thought of something. I have a couple of whitefish in the freezer. I think I'll make fish head soup out of them tomorrow. Rowena will just freak when she sees those big round eyes staring up at her from her soup bowl!"

"Abigail, you wouldn't!"

The old woman snickered. "I think you know me well enough by now, girlie, to realize just how nasty I can be when I'm ticked off!"

"Oh, yes, I know!" Meredith murmured, but Abigail didn't appear to hear her.

She paced the living room floor, her lined face pinched with frustration once more. "I certainly didn't want to leave those two alone in my house tonight since I don't trust them as far as I can throw them. Heaven knows what shenanigans they'll get up to when I'm not there! I swear Caleb was up to something no good this morning when Rowena and I were gone. He seemed mighty anxious to get the two of us out of the house, and I'm sure he must have been snooping because it looked like some of my stuff had been moved around. Damned nosy twit! Can't trust anybody nowadays, especially relatives! But if I have to hear him say one more time, '*Ooh, Aunt Abby, what a hoot you are*', I'm going to conk him over the head with my cast-iron frying pan! And that Rowena, she drives me crazy with her snooty attitude. Her nose is stuck so high up in the air, it's a wonder she hasn't drowned in the rain yet, or a bird hasn't used her nostrils for an outhouse!"

Meredith and I prudently remained silent and out of the way of the cross old woman, letting her vent her frustration and anger until she ran out of steam. My partner and I had learned the hard way that trying to reason with Abigail when she was in one of her "moods" was not always the wisest way to deal with her. Usually, the best tactic was to keep your mouth shut completely or to just nod and murmur in a noncommittal manner.

When it looked as though Abigail's tirade was in the process of winding down somewhat and her wrinkled cheeks seemed less flushed with irritation, Meredith said calmly, "Would you like a cup of tea now, Abby?"

The old woman plopped down on the sofa with a loud grunt. "Yes, and put a shot of rum in it, girlie. I need some fortification before I go back to those two annoying bozos."

As Meredith headed to the kitchen to get the tea, I padded over to the sofa and laid my head in Abigail's lap, gazing sympathetically up at her. After a sly look toward the kitchen, she ruffled my ears, her eyes losing some of their snappy fire. She dug into her jeans pocket and slipped me a piece of tasty jerky.

"Don't tell Meredith," she whispered. "She'll think I'm a nice person and we can't have that now, can we?"

Too late, I thought, happily munching on the treat. *Meredith already suspects you're not quite the ogre you want everyone to believe you are.*

Just as the second piece of jerky disappeared into my jaws, Meredith appeared with the tea tray and set it down on the coffee table in front of the sofa.

"Here we are!" she said, cheerfully, just as though there had never been a wild, ranting woman furiously pacing about her living room only a short time ago, turning the air blue with her unladylike curses.

Another way Meredith had of dealing with Abigail's crankiness was to simply ignore it and refuse to give the old woman the reaction she was hoping to provoke. It was not much fun if the victim of your acid-tongued remarks smiled sweetly at you instead of bursting into intimidated tears.

I could see the old lady visibly relaxing as she sipped her rum-laced tea and let herself be distracted by Meredith's tales of her day at work. Outside, the sun settled into the western horizon amid vivid flags of orange and red that reflected in the sparkling waters of the bay.

Meredith started to talk about our evening hike and I perked up, hoping she would mention Biggs and warn Abigail about him. Sure enough, my partner brought up the subject.

"There was this big, ugly guy in a black SUV driving like a maniac down the road earlier," Meredith said. "I didn't like the looks of him and neither did Flint. I'm not sure what he was up to, but I don't think it was anything good. He was asking all kinds of questions about how many people lived down this way. So, please be careful, Abigail, in case he comes around your place. He could have been casing the joint, looking for places to break into."

I gazed adoringly at my partner. *Casing the joint*. I just loved it when she talked like a hard-boiled detective!

"He was an inconsiderate slob, too," Meredith continued.

She reached into the pocket of her shorts and extracted the cigarette butt that Biggs had tossed at her feet. "He threw this out the window of his truck, which made me so mad. Why do people think they can just throw their garbage anywhere they like? If this had landed in some dry leaves or grass, it could have started a forest fire and burned the whole place down."

Abigail's eyes narrowed. "Let me see that."

Meredith handed her the butt, a curious look on her face at the tense note in the old woman's voice. Abigail examined the butt closely and then reached into the pocket of her shirt. I was happy to see she had not thrown out the cigarette butt I had shown her earlier that morning.

"Some creep in a big black vehicle nearly ran Rowena and me off the road on the way back to my place this morning," she said, her lips tightening. "And I found this butt by my front steps. It's the same brand as the one you just gave me. But Caleb said the guy was just someone who was lost. If that's true, why did he come back again tonight?"

Alarm slowly crept into Meredith's face. "Do you think Caleb knows this man and is lying for some reason about him being there?"

Abigail put her hands on her knees and pushed herself up off the sofa. Her mellow mood had vanished once more and her face looked like a thundercloud. "I'm darn well going to find out!" she grumbled.

Meredith rose, too. "Abby, please be careful. That man looked very shady and dangerous. If you see him hanging around your place, call the police immediately."

Abigail didn't answer, just strode purposefully toward the door and out into the darkening night. Meredith hurried after her, her face etched in worry as she watched the thin figure of the old woman disappearing down the deeply shadowed path toward her house.

Chapter 9

After Abigail's departure, I paced restlessly about the living room and jumped up on my chair several times to peer anxiously out the window into the darkness toward the old woman's invisible house. A strong sense of impending doom thrummed through my tense body. I couldn't help but worry that Abigail might have been rushing headlong into serious danger at home, especially if that criminal Biggs had shown up again.

My agitation finally prompted Meredith to put down the book she was trying to read and frown at me. "Flint, what in heaven's name is the matter with you? Why are you so restless? Do you have to go outside and pee?"

Ah, at last, an excuse to escape the confines of the house and rush over to Abigail's to make sure everything was okay. I jumped off the chair and padded quickly to the door, scratching lightly at its base.

"Okay, okay, hold your horses!" Meredith said, getting up quickly to open the door for me.

As I shot out into the warm, scented night amid a chorus of frog and cricket songs, she called after me, "Don't go too far! And watch out for bears and skunks!"

The thought of encountering a big, ferocious black bear or a stinky skunk in the darkness halted my headlong dash momentarily, but that concern was quickly overridden by worry for Abigail's safety. I had a good nose for trouble and what I smelled on the warm breeze that evening was big trouble spelled with the letters B-I-G-G-S.

I raced along the narrow path between our two properties, hoping I was wrong and I would arrive at Abigail's house to find her gaily concocting her fish head soup in the kitchen, while Caleb and Rowena sat gingerly on the edge of the sofa glaring at each other.

I slowed as Abigail's house came into sight. A light glowed in the kitchen window and I glimpsed a dark figure moving past it. It looked much too big to be any of the Tunners, but from that distance, it was hard to tell.

Warily, I crept closer, hearing the sound of a raised voice through the screen door as I neared the house. My hackles rose in apprehension. As I slipped quietly up the three steps in front of the kitchen door, I suddenly recognized the gravelly voice and stiffened in alarm. "Tell me where it is, old woman!"

Biggs!

A growl threatened to rumble out of my throat, but I stopped it just in time. I pressed myself against the side of the door and peeked around the edge.

The first thing I saw was Caleb and Rowena huddled against the big pine table. Caleb's thin face seemed paler than usual and he looked nervous, as though he was ready to jump out of his skin at any moment. Rowena, her frizzy straw hair piled in its usual topknot and bright red lipstick adorning her thin-lipped mouth, clutched Caleb's arm tightly, a look of stunned disbelief on her face.

As I watched uneasily, Caleb leaned forward and said in a voice that quivered slightly, "Aunt Abby, perhaps you should cooperate with this man. I really think he means business."

"Well, of course he means business, you idiot, or he wouldn't be holding a gun on me!"

Gun!

I tried to peer further around the doorframe without revealing my presence to the people in the kitchen and caught a glimpse of Abigail sitting stiffly in one of the kitchen chairs, her gray head tilted back and her eyes glaring at Biggs, who stood in front of her. I could clearly see the deadly black gun held in his enormous right hand, pointing straight at Abigail.

My heart thudded so loudly, I was sure the people inside the house would hear it. My instincts had been right after all. Abigail was in big trouble.

Biggs must have grown impatient waiting for Caleb and Rowena to find whatever money or jewels they thought Abigail had hidden in the house and decided to take matters into his own hands. His type of criminal always preferred the direct method of extorting information or cash out of people, which usually involved a gun or a weapon of some sort.

I turned my attention back to the tableau inside the brightly-lit kitchen as Caleb said pleadingly to Abigail, "Aunt Abby, please don't be stupid. Just give the man the money."

Abigail wore what I call her don't-mess-with-me-or-you'll-be-sorry look and her eyes flashed with fire. "He can shoot me if he wants to, but damned if I'm going to give him anything."

Caleb looked shocked. "Aunt Abby, you can't possibly mean that!" With fear in his eyes, his gaze shot toward Biggs. "The money is not worth your life. For heaven's sakes, just give it to him and he'll leave us alone."

"That's right, lady," Biggs spoke up. "Nobody will get hurt if you just hand over all the cash you got in the house."

"I don't have any cash in the house, and even if I did, I certainly wouldn't give it to the likes of you."

I winced slightly at the pugnacious tone of her voice. Abigail did not have a single cowardly bone in her skinny body, but I was afraid this time her belligerent attitude might provoke Biggs into dangerous action. Already, I could see that her resistance was causing his pockmarked face to redden with anger.

"Aunt Abby, don't be foolish," Caleb advised, urgently.

Abigail glared at him, her eyes narrowed. "You seem awfully anxious for me to give this creep all my money," she said, suspiciously. "What are you planning on doing, splitting it with him or what?"

Caleb jerked as though a bolt of lightning had struck him and his jaw dropped. Since I was well aware of his dastardly partnership with Biggs, I knew his look of outraged shock was totally false, although the nervous twitching was no doubt real. I didn't think Biggs holding Abigail at gunpoint and demanding the money had been part of the original plan, but Caleb was definitely up to his eyeballs in the nefarious scheme to rob his aunt of her rightful savings.

"Aunt Abby, what an awful thing to say! Are you implying that I know this man and I'm in on his plan to rob you? Why-Why, how can you even think such a horrible thing of your own flesh and blood? I'm totally hurt and devastated by your accusations! Rowena and I came up here hoping to have a nice visit with you and make up for all those years we haven't seen each other.

And now this man bursts into your house and demands your money, and you accuse *me* of helping him to rob you? I can't believe you would think that!"

He paused for breath, obviously trying hard to express righteous indignation, and I thought, *Methinks he doth protest too much!*

Abigail must have thought so, too, because she remained unmoved by his denials.

"What are you up to, Caleb?" she demanded. "Are you resorting to stealing from your own relatives now to maintain your lavish lifestyle instead of working honestly for a living?" She jerked her head toward Rowena, who so far had remained silent. "I guess it's hard to keep Her Highness here in expensive clothes and jewels and cars when you can't even hold a job for more than a year."

Rowena's face flushed an unbecoming red. "How dare you criticize *me*! At least I don't live in a shack in the middle of the bush and talk to the trees and rabbits," she snapped. "I've had enough of this crap! I don't have to stand here and take this."

She made as though to flounce out of the kitchen and Biggs waved the gun at her, his ugly face hardening like ice. "Nobody's going nowhere," he said, menacingly. "Until I get what I came here for, everybody stays put, understand?"

Rowena froze, her eyes staring apprehensively at the unwavering gun in the big man's hand.

Biggs grunted. "Now, all of you shut up. I'm sick of listening to you. Old lady, give me the money now, or I'll forget what a nice guy I am."

Abigail snorted. "Oh, yes, I'm sure your mother must be so proud of her saintly son."

Biggs' face darkened. "You have a smart mouth on you, old woman. One of these days, it's going to get you into big trouble."

"Hah! What trouble could possibly be worse than having a big, ugly galoot waving a gun in my face?" she scoffed. "It must make you feel real manly to intimidate a helpless little old lady and steal all her money."

I almost burst out laughing despite the extreme gravity of the situation. Helpless? Abigail was about as helpless as a 500-pound grizzly bear. When she got her dander up about something, nobody in his or her right mind wanted to tangle with her.

My amusement quickly died. Regardless of Abigail's tough-as-nails attitude, she still would be no match for Biggs if he decided to shut her smart mouth permanently. Not even her acidic, cutting tongue could deflect a speeding bullet headed for her brain or her heart. This was a situation that called for a little more tact and prudence on her part, but that was like asking a cougar to purr instead of growl.

Now that I had seen what the lay of the land looked like, so to speak, I decided it was time to bring my partner into the case. And the cops also needed to be called into action before the ugly situation deteriorated into a tragic mess.

Chapter 10

I padded silently down the steps and then took off like a rocket down the dark path. When I arrived home, I started barking frantically at the door to get Meredith's attention.

She opened it immediately, her face concerned. Right away, she knew something was wrong by the frenzied tone of my barks. "Flint, what's the matter?"

I dashed past her into the living room and over to the end table by her chair where her cell phone lay beside the book she had been reading. I grabbed the phone gently in my mouth and carried it over to her.

With a raised eyebrow, Meredith took the phone from me. "What in the world...?"

I didn't have time to answer her questions. Sprinting out into the night, I then doubled back to let her know I wanted her to follow me. I repeated this action a couple of times and, being the smart woman she was, she picked up on the message and hurriedly pulled the door closed behind her.

"Where are we going, Flint? What's wrong?" she demanded.

When I started down the narrow path toward Abigail's house, I heard her catch her breath behind me. "Is it Abigail? Has something happened to her?"

I woofed and ran faster. Meredith, bless her heart, knew me well enough to understand my dogese quite accurately most of the time, and thankfully, this was one of those times. She broke into a run behind me.

As we got closer to Abigail's house, I suddenly stopped, not wanting to rush in and give our presence away to the people in the house. Meredith, approaching behind me, almost tripped over my suddenly motionless body.

"Whoa, don't stop like that, Flint!"

She tried to edge around me to continue on, but I shifted to block her forward progress. Somehow, I had to impress upon her the need for stealth and quiet.

"Flint, move your butt! I need to find out if Abigail is all right."

I grabbed the cuff of her shorts in my jaws and tried to tug her firmly but slowly toward the log house. After a moment's resistance, she relented and followed me, her face reflecting puzzlement.

As we neared the kitchen steps, a man's angry voice thundered out into the night. "Look, lady, I've had just about enough from you! Give me the damn money now."

My heart lurched. Just as I feared, Biggs was quickly losing patience with the stubborn old woman of the house. At any moment now, he could start blasting away with that deadly gun of his.

At the sound of the gravelly, familiar voice, Meredith drew up short, and a small gasp escaped her. Her eyes widened in her shadowed face. "That sounds like that awful man in the SUV we saw earlier today!" she whispered. "What is *he* doing here?"

She pulled her shorts carefully out of my jaws and started toward the house. I was glad to see that she tiptoed quietly and tried to stay out of the light spilling from the kitchen window. As she pressed herself against the side of the house near the screen door, I moved silently beside her.

"You can't just shoot her in cold blood!" we heard Caleb say fearfully, and Meredith barely suppressed another shocked gasp. "Granted, she's a royal pain in the derriere, but the deal was only to take the money without anyone getting hurt."

"Aha!" Abigail pounced, triumphantly. "You just admitted you're part of the plan to rob me!"

"I never admitted any such thing," Caleb protested. "I'm just repeating what *he* said earlier."

"I've lived here for thirty years," Abigail said, her tone almost conversational. "I've never had a problem with anyone trying to break in or steal anything from me. Now you and Rowena come here for a surprise visit and, all of a sudden, some gangster waving a gun in my face is holding me hostage in my own kitchen. And this morning, you sent me on a totally useless trip into Sault Ste. Marie with Her Highness here while you no doubt snooped through my house and did heaven only knows what else. You lied to me when you said no one came to the house while I was gone. I know because this lout here dropped a cigarette butt by my front porch and nearly ran your wife and me off the road when we came back from the city. Now, try and deny all of that, Caleb Tunner."

A note of triumph infused her voice, and I could picture her leaning back in her chair, her sharp eyes pinning her nephew in an unrelenting glare.

"You're delusional, Aunt Abigail," Caleb blustered. "You've been living here alone in the bush for too long and you've gone squirrelly. Dad was right when he called you a nutty old hermit."

"Better a nutty old hermit than someone who would stoop so low as to try and steal from his own flesh and blood."

"Abigail, stop accusing us of being criminals!" Rowena screeched. "I'm sick and tired of being insulted and ridiculed by you. You're just a selfish, horrible old woman and you're going to get us all killed because you're too stubborn to see reason."

"Well, you've only got yourselves to blame for that," Abigail said, unrepentantly. "*I* certainly never invited you to visit, and *I* certainly had nothing to do with Bugsy Malone here threatening to shoot us all." She chuckled. "I guess it's true what they say about no honor among thieves, eh?"

Biggs interrupted Rowena's indignant spluttering, his rough voice weary. "I hate to break up this cozy family chat, but if I don't get the money in the next five minutes, nobody's going to be insulting nobody anymore."

I felt Meredith stiffen beside me and touch me lightly on the top of the head. I obeyed her silent signal to follow her down the steps and away from the house into the concealment of the trees at the edge of the property.

"Oh, my God, I can't believe this!" she whispered. "I *knew* that man was big trouble, but I never suspected that Caleb and Rowena might have come here to hurt Abigail."

She crouched in front of me and placed her hands on either side of my head, smiling into my eyes. "Good boy, Flint. I don't know how you knew Abigail was in trouble, but you're very clever for letting me know." Her forehead crinkled slightly. "And for making me bring my cell phone so I can call the police. Now that was kind of weird! But I've always said, Flint, that you're one smart pooch."

I stuck my tongue out and licked her cheek, quivering slightly in response to her compliment. Meredith was one of those rare humans who understood that dogs were far more than just bundles of shedding fur and drool that jumped on people and covered them with slobbery kisses. Yeah, okay, sometimes we *did* act like that, but we also possessed a lot more intelligence and comprehension skills than most people gave us credit for. Although, I had to admit I did sometimes turn into a wriggling, mushy mess when someone rubbed my belly and ears and called me a "sweet, adorable clown". It was awfully difficult to act dignified and intelligent in that kind of blissful situation.

Meredith dropped a quick kiss on top of my head and then stood up, fishing the cell phone out of her shorts pocket with a slightly shaking hand. I looked anxiously back toward Abigail's house as Meredith spoke in an urgent whisper into the phone.

When she clicked it shut, she put a hand on my head and peeked quickly in the direction of the house. "The dispatcher said there's a police unit out on Airport Road. They should be here in about ten minutes."

She nibbled her bottom lip. "God, I hope they're not too late! Poor Abigail, what did she ever do to deserve this?"

She snorted quietly with a trace of her normal wry humor. "Okay, okay, so she's not the nicest person in the world! She's rude and insulting and crabby. But she certainly doesn't deserve to be held at gunpoint in her own home, especially by her own relatives."

Technically, it was only Biggs holding the gun, but I knew what she meant.

Meredith tapped her foot restlessly, her arms crossed over her chest. Even though the evening was quite warm, she shivered slightly, her eyes focused on the square of light spilling from the kitchen window several meters away.

"I feel so helpless," she whispered. "I wish there was something I could do to help Abigail instead of just standing here waiting for the police."

My sentiments exactly, I thought, as I fidgeted by Meredith's side. Biggs sounded like he was dangerously close to the end of his patience, and I didn't doubt for a moment he would shoot Abigail in cold blood if she didn't hand over whatever money she had in the house. Ten minutes for the police to arrive might be ten minutes too late for the bad-tempered but irreplaceable old woman.

In a split second, I made up my mind. I couldn't sit idly by while my giver of secret treats faced such terrible danger alone. Before caution and common sense could weaken my resolve, I streaked toward the log house, dimly aware of Meredith calling after me in a frantic whisper to come back.

Chapter 11

Looking back on it later, I suppose it was probably foolhardy of me to react the way I did to the volatile situation in Abigail's house. The most sensible action would have been to wait for the police to arrive and let them handle it. There was no doubt this case was by far the most dangerous one I had so far faced, certainly much more serious than finding a missing child or an MP3 player. The consequences of my rash actions, as Meredith sternly pointed out to me afterward, could very well have been quite disastrous.

But at the time, all I could think of was that one of my pack members desperately needed my help. What kind of detective, and, more importantly, *friend*, would I have been if I didn't do everything in my power to help end her ordeal?

My protective instincts kicked into overdrive and I rushed to confront the criminals with slavering jaws and gnashing teeth. Okay, my jaws really weren't slavering, but I was definitely gnashing my teeth and hopefully looking as ferocious as a cute-faced Labrador retriever can.

With Meredith following frantically behind me, still trying to call me back in a fierce whisper, I raced up the kitchen steps and quickly nosed the screen door open. I squeezed through the narrow opening and burst into the brightly lit kitchen, causing the four people in it to turn to me with shocked faces.

Without hesitating, I headed straight for Biggs and sprang up to clamp my jaws tightly around the wrist of the hand holding the gun. He stumbled sideways, grunting in pain as my sharp teeth sank into his flesh.

Abigail was the first one to recover from my sudden appearance. She quickly stuck out her foot as Biggs staggered in front of her and the big man went flying, landing heavily and clumsily on the floor with me still clinging tenaciously to his arm. The gun went off with a loud bang, startling a high-pitched shriek out of Rowena and sending a bullet smashing into the ceiling overhead. The weapon flew through the air and landed with a thud by the big cook stove, and then skittered across the floor toward the sink.

Over by the table, Caleb and Rowena stood frozen, watching the action with almost identical looks of astonishment on their faces. Caleb recovered first, his pale face heating with fury.

"It's that mangy mutt again!" he shouted. "Get out of here, you fleabag!"

He made a move toward the gun lying by the stainless steel sink, but he didn't get very far. With a startled yelp and a hard thump, he found himself sitting on the floor on his skinny butt with a very angry Meredith looming over him.

"Oh, no, you don't!" she said, grinding out the words in cold, measured tones. Her eyes snapped with fire.

She stooped quickly and picked up the gun. Even though I knew she hated firearms with a passion and probably didn't even know how to fire one, she steadied it in both hands and pointed it as though she had been handling guns all her life.

"Nobody move," she ordered, in a stern voice that would have made Elliot Ness proud.

Biggs grunted and tried to pull his arm out of my jaws, but I clamped down harder, my throat vibrating with a menacing growl. Immediately halting further efforts to free himself, his mouth twisted in pain he couldn't quite conceal. I felt a thrill of satisfaction at having the gangster at my mercy, even though such drastic actions normally went against my friendly nature. He had threatened Abigail and that, in my opinion, thoroughly justified my rough treatment of him now.

Meredith flicked a quick glance toward the old woman. "Abby, are you all right?"

Abigail hoisted herself gingerly from the chair and stood with her hands on her hips, glowering at Caleb sprawled at her feet. "Yes, I'm fine, no thanks to my wonderful nephew here. If you and Flint hadn't come along when you did, Meredith, I'm sure Caleb would have let Al Capone shoot me in the head."

Caleb started to splutter, but Abigail cut him off sharply. "Oh, don't even bother, Caleb. You're only going to tell me more lies and I don't want to hear them. Tell them to the judge instead. Maybe he or she will believe you."

Rowena squeaked. Caleb's thin, pale face blanched as he stared at his aunt's rigid figure. "Surely you're not serious, Aunt Abby. You're not going to have me arrested, are you?"

"God, I knew this was a stupid idea!" Rowena bellyached. "Why the hell didn't you listen to me when I told you it was a stupid idea?"

"Shut up, Rowena!"

Her eyes flashed. "Don't tell me to shut up, you idiot! If you had just one ounce of brains in your stupid head, you wouldn't have gambled away all of our money in those stupid poker games and we wouldn't be in this predicament now."

"Oh, yeah? Well, if you didn't *spend* all of our money like it was going out of style on stupid clothes and stupid jewelry, I wouldn't have to get involved in those stupid poker games to try and win some of it back before you put us in the poorhouse!"

"*Me* put us in the poorhouse?" she screeched, her face twisted with rage. "I'm not the one with the gambling problem and the can't-keep-a-job-for-the-life-of-me problem. That would be you, bub."

Caleb sneered. "No, you're the one with the shop-till-you-drop problem. Who went out and bought that damn Lexus sitting outside that cost more than some people's houses, for God's sakes? Who has to strut around in Gucci and Armani and diamonds the size of ostrich eggs? That would be you, sister."

"Oh, sure, that's just like you, Caleb, to try and place all the blame on me! You weak, lily-livered..."

"If you both don't shut up right now, I will shoot you," Meredith told them.

Their verbal sparring subsided, but they continued to glare daggers at each other.

With one hand firmly holding the gun, Meredith fished the cell phone out of her pocket with the other and flipped it open, dialing 911 quickly. She told the police dispatcher that the man holding the gun had been disarmed and she now had possession of the weapon.

"Please tell the officers not to shoot me when they get here!" she begged.

Caleb started to rise from the floor, his face flushed with anger. "This is ridiculous! I'm not going to sit here and be insulted by both my wife and my aunt, who, by the way, is as batty as Dad always said she was."

"Sit down!" Abigail placed her foot in the middle of Caleb's skinny chest and shoved him forcibly back to the floor. He yelped and glared at her from his humiliating position at her feet. By now, all pretense of familial love had fled him and only sullen dislike and contempt shone from his eyes.

The old lady's face remained stony and cold. "Why shouldn't I have you arrested?" she demanded. "You may be related to me by blood, which, unfortunately, I can't do anything about, but damned if I'm going to let you get away with trying to steal from me and letting this mobster invade my home. You're a disgrace to the Tunner name, Caleb. I always knew you were useless, but I never thought you would stoop this low."

"We weren't going to *steal* the money," Caleb said, sullenly. "Just—*borrow* it temporarily until I could get another job. I figured you'd never miss it, anyway, living the way you do here like an old hermit. Hell, the money's probably been moldering away under your mattress for years now." His thin mouth twisted. "I knew you'd never just lend me the money if I asked you for it."

Abigail's lips tightened. "So you figured you'd just force your way into my home for a cozy little visit and then waltz back to Toronto with all my hard-earned money stashed in your fifty pieces of luggage. And I would be none the wiser 'cause I'm just a batty old lady."

"I would have paid it back!" Caleb insisted.

The old woman snorted. "Of course you would have. Being the fine, honest, upstanding citizen you are."

Caleb opened his mouth, but whatever he was going to say remained unspoken as one uniformed police officer burst into the kitchen from the living room and another came charging through the back door, guns drawn. Both shouted, "Police! Don't move!" at the same time, and their voices ricocheted through the tense atmosphere in the room.

One officer, a good looking young man with black curly hair and brilliant blue eyes, turned his immediate attention toward Meredith, who stood frozen with Biggs' revolver still pointed toward him lying on the floor. While keeping his own weapon trained carefully on Meredith, the officer held out his left hand.

"Miss Steele, I presume? Please give me the weapon now, ma'am."

Meredith obeyed immediately. She gingerly placed the gun in the man's outstretched hand and then snatched her own hands away as though the revolver had suddenly turned into a fanged serpent. She looked pale and shaken as delayed reaction began to set in.

What a sight we must have looked, I thought, as I finally loosened my grip on Biggs' wrist now that reinforcements had arrived. Two men sprawled in rather undignified positions on the floor, one with a growling black dog attached to him, a little old lady who looked as ferocious and dangerous as a cornered wolverine, a heavily made-up cavewoman in a red silk dress and an expression of petulant sullenness, and a pretty young woman in shorts and a halter top holding a huge revolver in a wide-legged stance like a heroine in an action flick.

No wonder the two police officers seemed slightly dazed by the tableau in Abigail's kitchen. Meredith's first frantic 911 call had no doubt left them with the expectation of encountering a tense situation in which they would have to disarm the gangster Biggs and take him down before he could shoot anyone. Instead, the situation had already been diffused and the suspects were ready to be taken into custody.

Before I left Biggs and moved to press myself tightly against the trembling Meredith, I shoved my face close to the big man's ugly mug and growled deeply to let him know that if he tried anything funny, I would gladly sink my teeth into other parts of his anatomy. Satisfaction was mine when I saw him flinch slightly from my rather impressive canines, and wisely, he remained where he was, his ugly face unmovable as granite as he realized the jig was up.

The older of the two police officers scrutinized each of us in turn, raised his eyebrows, and said in a flat voice, "Now, will someone please tell us what the hell is going on here?"

Chapter 12

While Meredith and Abigail tried to explain the situation amid loud protestations from Caleb and Rowena, another police cruiser skidded into Abigail's driveway, lights flashing and siren howling. Two officers, this time a man and a woman, bounded up the front steps and into the house.

The woman officer took in the scene in the kitchen and addressed the officer who had taken the gun from Meredith. "Is everything under control, Jake?"

He nodded. "Three suspects to take into custody and nobody hurt." Whereupon, he proceeded to sternly lecture Meredith on the foolhardiness of her actions in attempting to alleviate the situation herself instead of waiting for the police. She looked properly chastened and sent me a quelling look. My gaze slid guiltily away from hers, but at the same time, I felt a certain satisfaction in having prevented Abigail from being gunned down in cold blood.

"Now listen here, young man," Abigail spoke up, sharply. "If Meredith had not intervened when she did, this goon would have shot me in the head without a second thought. You should be giving her a medal of commendation instead of blasting her for doing something any half-decent human being would have done."

The police officer seemed unfazed by the old woman's anger. "That may be true, ma'am," he said, mildly. "But nevertheless, we like to discourage people from taking the law into their own hands. It can be very dangerous."

"Believe me! I'll try very hard not to do it again," Meredith promised, fervently.

As Caleb was being handcuffed, he looked beseechingly over his shoulder at Abigail. "Aunt Abby, tell them this is all a mistake! Biggs is the one who should go to jail, not Rowena and me. We didn't do anything."

Abigail gazed at him impassively. "Maybe a stint in the hoosegow will smarten you up a bit, Caleb. Don't expect me to bail you out."

She turned her back on him, raising her chin haughtily, but not before I saw a brief flash of hurt disappointment in her eyes. Despite her apparent shortage of love for her nephew, it must have still been upsetting to think that her own relative would go to such nefarious lengths to steal money from her.

As the three culprits were led away in handcuffs to the police cruisers parked in Abigail's driveway, Biggs maintained a surly silence and stared straight ahead. Not so Caleb and Rowena, who alternately railed at each other, Biggs, Abigail and the whole uncaring, unfair universe in general.

Joe and Linda Ford, along with Geordie, came rushing up just as the doors of the cruisers slammed shut, cutting off the younger Tunners' strident voices.

"Abigail, Meredith, what the heck is going on?" Linda exclaimed. "We heard the police cars go racing by our place a few minutes ago. Is everyone all right? What happened?"

Meredith threw a quick glance at Abigail. "Someone tried to rob Abby," she explained, obviously reluctant to say that two of the culprits were the old woman's own relatives.

Linda's eyes widened. "Oh, my God, Abigail, are you all right?"

She threw her arms around the old lady, who stiffened and pulled away, her eyes snapping. "I'm fine, I'm fine! Quit fussing over me."

Linda laughed. "Yeah, you're definitely okay."

Geordie was full of excited questions, but I hushed him. Tomorrow would be soon enough for explanations. Right now, I wanted nothing more than to go home, jump on my chair and sleep for a day. This case had worn me out and, like Meredith after she had gotten rid of Biggs' dangerous weapon, I was beginning to feel the adrenaline draining away and reaction setting in.

The older officer, who said his name was Dave Madigan, asked Meredith and Abigail to come to the police station in the morning to have their statements taken, and then he and the other officers drove off into the night with the three culprits. I swore I could still hear Rowena's screeching voice long after the cars had disappeared out of sight.

Meredith wanted to stay with Abigail for the rest of the night, or at least have her come home with us, but she adamantly refused. Meredith conceded reluctantly and we trudged back home, both of us exhausted from the night's work.

The next evening, Meredith and Abigail sat on the deck of our house while I lolled in the grass by the water's edge, gnawing on a tasty rawhide chew. Abigail once again sipped a cup of tea laced with rum, a sure indication that yesterday's events had affected her more than she was willing to admit, while Meredith enjoyed a glass of red wine.

"I still can't believe it," Meredith said, shaking her head. "Things like this just don't happen here in Gros Cap."

Abigail grunted. "Then you and I both must have had a bad dream last night, girlie. I know that big ugly galoot Biggs sure looked like something out of a nightmare."

She gave Meredith an inquiring glance. "What made you come over to my place, anyway? How did you know something was going on?"

Meredith gave me a fond smile. "Actually, it was Flint who told me."

Abigail's gray eyebrows rose skeptically. "Flint the dog?"

Meredith laughed. "How many other Flints do you know? Somehow he sensed you were in trouble and persuaded me to come with him to your house. He even made me bring my cell phone so I could call the police."

The old woman gazed at me with a curious expression on her wrinkled face. "Detective Flint at work again, eh? You know, he's the one who showed me the cigarette butt by my front porch. I might never have seen it if he hadn't pointed it out to me."

"And he knew that Biggs character was big trouble," Meredith remarked. "I've never seen him take such an instant dislike to anyone before."

She studied Abigail, her pretty face sympathetic. "It must have been quite a shock to find out that Caleb intended to steal from you, Abby. After all, he *is* family."

The old woman's face twisted sourly. "Don't remind me! Considering that Ronald is his father, it doesn't come as a big surprise to me that my nephew is no better than a common thief and a stupid one to boot. As they say, the apple doesn't fall far from the tree. Just to show you what a dysfunctional family he comes from, I called Ronald last night to tell him what happened. And would you believe it? He had the nerve to blame *me* for Caleb and Rowena being arrested! Said if I wasn't so stingy and selfish with my money and such a stubborn, cantankerous old woman, they should have been able to come to me for help. And because they're family, I should have gladly given it to them. Then they wouldn't have had to resort to stealing. What a bunch of malarkey! And Minnie was just as bad. I could hear her screeching in the background about what a horrible old woman I was to have her precious baby arrested."

"And what did you say?" Meredith asked, smiling.

Abigail snorted. "First of all, I asked Ronald, since he was so concerned about family responsibility, why *he* hadn't given his only son money to help him out of his financial woes. My fool of a brother started blustering and blubbering about how he didn't know Caleb was in such serious trouble, at which point I asked him how the hell he expected *me* to know then, since I hadn't see the boy in heaven knows how many years? Not surprisingly, he didn't have an answer for that. And then he went on and on about how money was a little tight nowadays and the cost of living in Mississauga was so high and the used car business was kind of slow, and blah, blah, blah. I finally told him he was a brainless idiot and his fool of an offspring was his problem, not mine. Then I hung up on him."

"Good for you," Meredith said, obviously holding no sympathy for the two people who had caused so much trouble. Or for Ronald either, who it appeared probably deserved much of the acidic criticism heaped on him by his sister.

"What I don't understand is why would Caleb and Rowena think you have so much money stashed away in your house?" Meredith asked. She laughed. "Did they really think you had thousands of dollars hidden under your mattress?"

I paused in my chewing for a moment, recalling a remark Caleb had made to Biggs when they were searching the house about something being hidden under a mattress. It struck me as odd at the time, but now it made sense.

I perked up my head as a sheepish expression crossed Abigail's face.

Meredith peered more closely at her. "Abigail Tunner, don't tell me you *do* have money stashed under your mattress!"

"Don't be ridiculous," she snapped. "That's the first place a thief would look. I'm not that stupid."

She paused and Meredith's eyes widened with incredulity. "But you do have money hidden somewhere else in your house?"

Abigail sipped furiously at her tea and refused to answer. Meredith could only shake her head in disbelief. "But how in the world did Caleb and Rowena know you had a secret stash of cash?"

The old lady snorted. "From my moronic brother, I suppose. In one of our rare phone calls a while back, he was bragging about how well off he was and telling me how poor and destitute I was living up here in the bush."

"But I thought he told you last night he didn't have any money to help Caleb."

Abigail snorted again. "That shows you just how much of a dimwit he is. He can't even keep his own lies straight. And being a used-car salesman in Toronto doesn't exactly put him in the same league as Bill Gates. Anyway, I got sick and tired of listening to his phony baloney and told him I had more money and jewelry hidden under my mattress than the Queen of England had in her vaults. I guess he must have mentioned it to Caleb and Rowena and they believed it. That must be why they hatched this harebrained scheme to come up here and steal it. Or, *borrow* it, as Caleb tried to claim."

Meredith shook her head sadly. "It's unbelievable what some people will do for money. Considering that Caleb and Rowena didn't actually steal anything and it was Biggs who threatened you with the gun, I'm sure your nephew and his wife will get off pretty lightly. But I just hope they've learned their lesson and won't do anything so stupid again."

"I wouldn't count on it," Abigail muttered. "But as long as they stay away from me, I don't care what they do."

Meredith's lips twitched in amusement. "Oh, I'm pretty sure you won't be seeing much of those two in the near future! Not after their harrowing experience in the wilds of Northern Ontario with the 'crazy old lady of Gros Cap'."

Abigail chortled and I grinned as I gnawed on the tasty piece of rawhide.

Meredith was right. It was highly unlikely that Caleb and Rowena Tunner would ever trouble Abigail again. Laboring under the delusion that she was a helpless, loony old woman had been their biggest mistake and the cause of their downfall. I was pretty sure they would stay as far away as possible from her in the future.

Epilogue

Abigail bounced back pretty quickly after her ordeal at the hands of that goon Biggs and her nefarious nephew Caleb. Despite the old lady's dire threats to leave Caleb and Rowena to rot indefinitely in the hoosegow, she subsequently dropped the charges against them on the condition that they never darken her doorway again. Needless to say, they emphatically agreed and high-tailed it back to Toronto as though all the hounds of Hell were chasing after them.

The gangster Biggs, on the other hand, did end up with major jail time for his part in the attempted armed robbery—and, I might add with some satisfaction, several stitches in his wrist from a certain canine's sharp teeth. His incarceration in the prison system was no great loss to society as I saw it. I wasn't sure what his boss Mr. Connelly thought of his goon enforcer being brought down by a feisty old lady and a black lab, but I didn't imagine he was overly impressed.

Abigail's brother Ronald and his wife Minnie refused to have anything further to do with the old woman after she had Caleb and Rowena arrested; a state of affairs that didn't seem to faze her in the slightest. There was definitely no love lost on either side of that familial relationship.

As for me, *The Mattress Affair*—as I had decided to call the case—was barely solved and put to rest, and already I was wondering what Flint and Steele's next case would be.

THE END

ABOUT THE AUTHOR

Cheryl Landmark lives in a quiet, picturesque hamlet called Gros Cap in Northern Ontario, Canada, with her husband, Mike, and faithful canine companion. She loves dogs, reading, jigsaw puzzles, and, of course, writing novels and poetry in her spare time.

She is also the author of two fantasy novels called WIND AND FIRE and POOL OF SOULS and a young adult adventure called SHADOWS IN THE BROOK.

Visit her website at: www3.sympatico.ca/cheryl.landmark

Made in the USA
Charleston, SC
01 August 2014